Parallax is Robin Morgan's fourth novel. She has published seven poetry collections (including her recent *Dark Matter*), and eleven books of nonfiction on social justice issues, primarily feminism, including her now-classic *Sisterhood* anthologies. She is a grantee of the U.S. National Endowment for the Arts, and a recipient of numerous other awards. Her work has been widely translated. An activist in the global Women's Movement for decades, recognized as a leading architect of U.S. feminism, and a former Editor-in-Chief of *Ms.* magazine, she co-founded The Sisterhood Is Global Institute with Simone de Beauvoir and co-founded The Women's Media Center with Jane Fonda and Gloria Steinem.

www.RobinMorgan.net
www.facebook.com/TheRobinMorgan/
Twitter @TheRobinMorgan

D1113128

Also by Robin Morgan

Poetry
Dark Matter: New Poems
A Hot January: Poems 1996–1999
Upstairs In The Garden: Selected And New Poems
Depth Perception
Death Benefits
Lady Of The Beasts
Monster

Fiction
The Burning Time
Dry Your Smile
The Mer Child

Nonfiction
Fighting Words: A Toolkit For Combating The Religious Right
Saturday's Child: A Memoir
The Word Of A Woman
The Demon Lover: The Roots Of Terrorism
A Woman's Creed
The Anatomy Of Freedom
Going Too Far

Anthologies (Assigned, Compiled, Edited, and Introduced)
Sisterhood Is Forever
Sisterhood Is Global
Sisterhood Is Powerful
The New Woman (Co-Ed.)

PARALLAX

A Novel

Robin Morgan

First published by Spinifex Press, 2019

Spinifex Press Pty Ltd
PO Box 5270, North Geelong, VIC 3215, Australia
PO Box 105, Mission Beach, QLD 4852, Australia

women@spinifexpress.com.au
www.spinifexpress.com.au

Cover design by Deb Snibson, MAPG
Typesetting by Helen Christie, Blue Wren Books
Typeset in Berling
Printed by McPherson's Printing Group

 A catalogue record for this
book is available from the
National Library of Australia

ISBN: 9781925581959 (paperback)
ISBN: 9781925581980 (ebook: epub)
ISBN: 9781925581966 (ebook: pdf)
ISBN: 9781925581973 (ebook: kindle)

For the inheritors ...

CONTENTS

par·al·lax
/ˈper-ə-laks/
noun

The effect whereby the position or direction of an object appears to differ when viewed from different positions.

AUTHOR'S NOTE

One citizen of the universe is a small creature who as a matter of course transforms itself through four distinct lives within four distinct existences.

The Monarch is sometimes called the 'milkweed butterfly', since the underside of milkweed leaves is the only food its larvae can eat. Monarchs and related species are found wherever milkweed's own plant relatives, sometimes called Bloodflowers, grow—on every continent except the polar regions.

The plant protects its butterfly.

'Milk' ingested by a larva renders the Monarch poisonous to birds of prey. In the intricate balance requiring fairness to predators, however, the flicker of black-banded, tangerine Monarch wings signals that this prey may be toxic. Then again—a sly counter to simplistic assumptions—not all Monarchs are poisonous, since not all milkweeds produce noxious juices. Yet the butterfly's warning still performs a witty camouflage for poisonous and non-poisonous Monarchs alike, arming both against birds of prey. And—because life imitates not only art but itself—the innocently non-toxic Viceroy butterfly mimics the colors and patterns of the Monarch, sending the same alert, gaining the same protection. The wings of both butterflies—all butterflies, in fact—collect energy from sunlight to stay warm: they reap the light.

The Monarch, apparently unsatiated by these gaudy carnival masks of color, reinvents itself ceaselessly, shifting through four discrete lives in a single existence, and paying the price exacted by such metamorphoses—with repeated death throes and relentless resurrections.

The miniscule eggs laid on the underside of milkweed leaves take three to five days to hatch into tiny larvae, who begin sucking at the leaves. Over the next two weeks, each larva elongates into a black-striped worm the color of young limes, capable of spinning threads from itself. It weaves these into a sheath, then wreaths its body inside this chrysalis, the cocoon where it dangles for another lifetime, ten days. Finally, with the violence characteristic of any organism writhing free from old forms, what had been a caterpillar emerges—wet, matted, unrecognizable. Until wings shudder open and spread, harvesting light, drying, into perfect miniature stained-glass windows the hues of sunrise and midnight: an adult Monarch.

Then it steps onto air and flies.

Whether it remembers or cares who it was before flight is a matter of speculation, but only among humans.

This last lifetime aloft can be as short as fourteen or as long as forty days, during which time it might mate, might lay eggs. Then it dies.

Well, not quite.

These quatrefoil lives on a single stem parallel four existences in one discrete life—four generations in a single year—which the Monarch requires for survival.

The first generation, born in late winter, perishes after having laid eggs for the next. The second generation, born in late spring, does the same. So does the third, born in midsummer.

All three develop, creep, suck, grow, spin, weave, wrap, dangle, writhe, shudder, spread, fly, mate, spawn, and die. All three follow the same quartile cycle: larva, caterpillar, chrysalis, butterfly.

But the fourth generation is different.

The fourth generation, born in autumn, does not die after fourteen days, or even forty.

The fourth generation migrates. It flies for three months—over oceans, through storms, lightning, snows, predators, beating wings filmy as petals—almost three thousand miles. No other insect can fly such a distance. Once the Monarchs recognize as home the roosting place where they have never been, they land.

The fourth generation rests in this warmth for as long as eight months, hibernating in clusters, each Monarch slowing its heart rate until internal time turns on the annual axis of light.

Then up to two-thirds of this generation emerges, twice-born, to mate, lay eggs, and then die. From those eggs, life-stage-one of the first generation begins.

The last third of the old generation? Re-emerging, twice-born, it starts the journey back—great glowing blizzards of wings swarming and mating in the hundreds of thousands—resting along the way in stages, spawning, dying. A new generation then takes to the air for as long as three months—across oceans, through heat, rain, winds, predators, beating and beating wings filmy as petals—almost three thousand miles. Once the Monarchs recognize as home the place where they have never been, they land. There it begins again.

Whether at any point the Monarch views its current stage as a position or a direction—as the whole or as a part of the whole—is not known. That may also differ when viewed from the different perspectives themselves: a parallax.

There are theories about why the Monarch migrates. But no one knows for sure. There are studies of the migratory patterns. But the routes change.

The migration takes up to three generations to complete. Only one thing is known for certain.

No one butterfly ever makes the round trip.

PARALLAX

THE YARNER

The Yarner lived in the oldest section of the City, a vast metropolis, capital of the Trust. Inside its massive walls, spires of stone loomed like perched raptors clawing at the eastern edge of the continent, eyes aglitter, glaring out at the world. An island universe, the City leaned into the wind's roar and ocean storms when they battered the coast.

The old part of the City was different.

Here the cobbled streets were narrow and quiet, laid along the winding rural dirt lanes they had been only thirty centuries earlier. Here trees still grew, some even taller than the squat old buildings that leaned tipsily, stone-smoothed by age, above long-since-shifted foundations.

Here, at the end of an alleyway, lived the Yarner, in a small house that boasted as its sole distinction the flowering pear tree out front. Here, in mild weather, the Yarner could be found sitting on the stoop, watching the light change, feeding breadcrumbs to the finches, and sometimes, if in the mood when importuned, feeding a story to a hungry listener.

There were few such listeners now, and virtually no hunger—at least in the City, where urbanians had outgrown the inconvenience of seasons. Year round, the farthest provinces and colonies sent their tribute to the capital: taxes, information, delicacies. Provincials might grow but not sample succulent fruits reserved for export to urban markets, so that city servants might offer their employers summer's ripeness throughout the winter. Villagers might huddle in freak ice-storms, fall from stroke during heat-waves, or watch their shanties sink beneath rising floodwaters, but here at the heart of power the temperature was sufficiently tamed—fires stoked and fans wielded by servants—to permit the donning of thin woolen wraps in summer, silk shifts in winter. Villagers might be grateful to wear caravan-sold cheap garments inked with images of famous City athletes and performers, but their own crafts—intricate needlework, glazed earthenware, vivid hand-woven fabrics—were exported for purchase in the cities, where sophisticates appreciated them in ways their makers could not.

The Trust's citizens prided themselves on being open to new ideas and sensations. Yet they were exhausted. They had become a people of large-bodied individuals whose hearts stuttered under the weight of their flesh, so sated with indulgence that even their children were oversized and despondent. Furthermore, since both children and adults were continually being informed, everyone knew everything but recalled nothing. As a consequence, they had no need for stories invented as imagination, only for stories invented as fact.

Instead, they had three obsessions: their work, not for love for it but because they were certain their possessions, thus lives, depended on it; their anxieties—about loss, pain, ageing, death, bad dreams, crowds, loneliness, strangers, and appearing strange to others; and last, their boredom—they yearned not to be sated any more, so they had appetite only for one thing: hunger.

But they were an efficient people.

They sought quick, practical solutions to their needs, and the invention and procurement of such solutions in turn fostered the Trust's growth, enriching it further and presenting the lives of its citizens, particularly urbanians, as the envy of aspiring colonials. The solutions were numerous, competitive, and easily purchased across a range of prices, though none were cheap. Procedures to plane the body slender; to sleeken, soften, or firm the flesh. Techniques to sleep serenely, wake energetically, think pragmatically. Fuels to heighten feeling but block pain, to excite the spirit, calm or cheer the emotions, sharpen the mind, expedite physical and spiritual grace, accelerate acquisition of wisdom, and delay growing old. These were busy people. They sought out experts whose skills could help them accomplish their aspirations more swiftly and successfully. For this, they would spare no cost. For other experiences they could spare no patience. Thus few had any appetite for stories, certainly not for stories that resisted unfolding rapidly in a violent arousal of the senses, stories that were not useful.

One day, a stranger appeared near the front stoop of the little house at the end of the alleyway in the oldest part of the City that was the capital of the Trust. He moved as if the precise moment in space he inhabited hung poised before the infliction of time, where it was always Now. He crawled toward the stoop on his hands and knees.

In reality he stood upright, though he did walk hesitantly. But an attentive observer would have noticed he was crawling.

"This will do," he muttered to no one.

The Yarner perched on the stoop peered at him—eyes

raking a slow sweep from his faded green cap down the half-hidden face to the shabby clothing, gaunt body, battered knapsack with the curved neck of a five-string doola'h sticking out, down to the worn straps of his sandals—taking in every detail before deciding to comprehend the words that had been coming out of his mouth. The stranger was claiming to have traveled great distances in search of tales told rarely or no longer told at all. He had heard about this Yarner more than once and had followed that trail, but now seemed unsure he had found the right destination.

The Yarner studied the stranger, then coughed, spat, and spoke.

"When you look at me, you see an old woman. Don't be deceived."

The stranger squatted down, then settled in two steps lower on the stoop, leaning against his knapsack.

"I killed my first man before I was born," the Yarner continued, placidly.

The stranger nodded in respect.

"That's not easy."

"Easy enough. Having got my mother with child, my father fled. He'd been running all his life, poor man. But after that, he couldn't stop, not ever, really. He died haunted by memories misshapen by time, never feeling safe from whatever he feared was tracking him. He wondered if it was me. In truth, I was engrossed with forgetting him."

The stranger nodded again.

"Why have you a taste for stories?" The Yarner asked abruptly, sifting the ravel of wools pooled in her lap, "Nobody wants stories now."

The stranger folded his hands. They were large, gnarled hands, but the fingers were slender and tapered. He stared at those hands.

"I can't remember," he finally said.

"Hah … Long time on the journey, eh." It wasn't a question.

"Yes."

"Not many of you left." She squinted at him. "Not many of me, neither."

"All the more reason."

"Hah." She reversed her knitting needles and began a new row. "Not so simple as some might think. Yarns get frayed or broken, you know. Telling gets interrupted. Sometimes interruptions *are* the story. And every second, stories unfold all over the place. Some unfold as they're happening, some haven't happened yet, some never will—and that turns out to be the story. There's tiny stories nested inside bigger stories nested inside epic … oh, way out past infinity. Can make a person dizzy." Her fingers flashed, looping and twining whorls of magenta and indigo. "See, there, the pear tree? Well, there's the story of the pear tree: who planted it and why, here at the end of this alleyway; how it grew, even in this City; how it buds, flowers, fruits … clearly, there's that story. But what about the story of each leaf? Each unique leaf as it unfurls, flickers in the wind a thousand times maybe, and now, when autumn's pruning the light, brittles into brightness, lets go, falls—and flies? Or the stories about what views the sparrows see, what sounds they hear and thoughts they mull, balancing on the boughs? Or the story of that twisted left branch? What about the story of the pear-tree's roots, the story of its dark, moist soil, and the multitude of unseeable creatures swarming there? Every yarn is made of strands, every story of worlds that can never ever be told, since no one could live long enough to spin them. Or hear them. And they *keep* unfolding, too, continuously, simultaneously, skeins living along the same yarn. You can spot one at a time and sometimes, very rarely, you can glimpse a multitude swarming—though no yarner can ever see both the individual tale and the swarm at the same moment. It's enough to strike any teller silent, dumbfounded with awe."

The stranger's eyes darkened.

"Oh, don't worry, I'll feed you what I have. Never turned anybody away—well, almost never … and an offer of two weeks' board in advance, after all. Besides, just because something can't ever be done doesn't mean yarners don't keep trying, generation after generation. Power, curse, gift, whatever it is, we learn to own it. Might as well, since it owns us. We know we can always give up later—just not yet." She shifted her weight and grunted. "So we set out, again and again, no idea where we're going though we always get someplace we recognize when we arrive, though we've never been there. But I warn you. My words snarl and purl. The yarns I keep have patterns. They overlap, contradict, reinforce. They *knit*." Then, suddenly cross, she added, "Don't think I have time to point out these patterns as I go. You can ignore them or forget them or pay attention. But if you're one of those who feel you can't wait out the silence, don't expect me to do your listening for you."

The stranger nodded, not daring to smile.

The Yarner blinked at him, snorted, spat again, and wiped her nose on her sleeve. Then, with no pretense of reluctance, she began.

THE EMBODIMENT

Back when there were kingdoms and wars, wars were regarded as crucial for building and strengthening kingdoms. But over time they became too costly in lives and treasure, and began to erode the justifications for their existence. As kingdoms weakened, monasteries gradually began absorbing what had been government functions.

At first this arose from the monks' genuine concern that in the absence of effective administration, the people's basic needs—health, education, order, trade, and such—were not being met. Since the monks led structured lives and weren't corrupt, they seemed the natural sector of society to shoulder such tasks in this emergency.

But as they addressed increasingly complex and burdensome issues the monks, being human, naturally began to confuse the good of the people with the good of the monks. At the central monastery, where the Tiktaalik, the chief abbot, lived, they began debating how to perpetuate their status, how to fix what had been a temporary resolution into a permanent one.

It was not simple. For example, the monks knew that they could not entertain any dynastic option. They were celibate, and would not consider imperiling their purity by changing their rules. So there was no chance of the Tiktaalik siring his successor. Yet they also felt strongly that they could not risk sharing the burden of authority with those outside the monastic community.

It was Tiktaalik Naamuro who devised the system that the monks, and in time the populace, would come to call The Return.

The Return was what people nowadays would call a reincarnation belief. But such a belief was not yet practiced in that time and region, so it wore a powerful mystique, appearing new and revelatory. The soul of the Tiktaalik would, upon his death, return to the material dimension and transfer itself to live again in the body of a newborn boy. Once recognized as the Embodiment, the infant would, after three years, be taken from his family and raised by the monks. Such families were to feel themselves greatly honored. The fathers exclaimed loud praise at receiving blessings and monetary remuneration for the loss of a son. The mothers were usually struck wordless and tearful by the depth of their gratitude.

The problem of dynasty was thus solved: the Tiktaalik would in effect succeed himself.

The system held during the reigns of those Tiktaaliks elected in the traditional manner by the monks during interim periods when boys who embodied The Return needed time to grow and be trained. Only Tiktaaliks whose souls were highly advanced (as decided by later Tiktaaliks) could endure the ordeal of Returning. Otherwise, any monks—even common people—might go about transferring their souls around at will.

The populace was not ready for this, the monks decided, any more than the populace was equipped to share the monastic privilege of electing its own leadership.

This system endured well enough, though only for eight or so hundred years.

Then, something happened.

The ritual by which the Embodiment could be recognized began to change.

For centuries, the monks had located the rare newborn who was the Embodiment through various signs pointing to his whereabouts: a comet or star shooting through the night sky; a pregnant woman reporting strange dreams; birthmarks interpreted as symbols; and a perceptible precocity in the child, evidenced by his appearing familiar with details of a deceased Tiktaalik's life. All this had become fairly standard. It never occurred to anyone to violate tradition, either by ignoring signs or falsifying them. Thus was a balance preserved in faithful observance by both the monks and the people, and order was maintained.

As the monastery's power increased, however, the lot of the people failed to improve. One year, severe drought and subsequent near-famine wracked the land, and many succumbed to sickness and starvation, drifting to their deaths like wintery leaves—wisps of what they once had been. The monks grieved. But it was imperative that they hoard food for themselves in monastery storehouses, because they dare not go hungry or fall ill. Without them, the government could not function and society might descend into chaos.

Then, with the first rains, as people were just beginning to recover from the disaster, an astonishing proliferation of signs began to appear.

On any given morning, six or seven pregnant women would present themselves at the monastery gates to report strange dreams. At least twice a week, a father would appear, carrying his son, who bore peculiar birthmarks. Sometimes an entire family would request an audience with the current chief abbot, Tiktaalik Yimnaamik, pleading that he test their young son with questions about the life of a previous Tiktaalik.

When this phenomenon began, the people interpreted it as a celebratory omen confirming the end of drought and famine. The monks saw it as a blessing affirming their decisions, in the benevolent form of so many Returns by former leaders.

But as crowds at the monastery outer gates grew larger and interviews demanded more of their attention, the monks became distressed. There was little time for the business of state, even less for meditation. Their serenity felt violated. Pregnant women squatted heavily on swollen ankles, chatting in soft voices, in the outer courtyard. Fathers jostled other fathers to reach or remain at the front of the queue. Once inside the monastery, wee claimants crawled or tottered over the polished stone floors, smearing puddles or worse in their wake, making the halls smell nothing like incense. The smaller the persons, the louder their wails for their mothers, insistent shrieks piercing the hum of what once had been steady, soothing chants.

Something had to be done.

One day, a woman already known to the monks presented herself, carrying her young child. Her name was Lobaa, and she was familiar because she was that rare creature: the offspring of a Tiktaalik. Her father, Lobaak, had been a township scribe who entered monastic orders late in his life—after having been married, siring a child, and burying his wife. Grieving, he had tended to, then later been tended to by, his growing daughter. Lobaak had a quiet, meditative mind, so becoming a monk was for him a smooth transition, and in time he proved himself such a valued member of the community that he was elected Tiktaalik.

Being the offspring, even if only the daughter, of a Tiktaalik was special indeed. To be sure, Lobaa was never permitted access to the inner rooms of the monastery, but she was allowed to serve Tiktaalik Lobaak almost as she had served him before he had become a monk.

She baked the fig pastries he so enjoyed and brought them to the monastery, leaving them at the inner courtyard gates. She wove the special blue and gold cloth donned by the Tiktaalik on grand holidays. She swept the outer courtyards and tended the vegetable and herb gardens, the sole female privileged to work alongside local men employed for this purpose. She was even permitted to continue these labors after her father died and was succeeded by another Tiktaalik—this one also elected, there being at that time no Embodiment old enough to ascend to power.

But all these favors were abruptly withdrawn when it was noticed that her belly had begun to swell.

Surprisingly, Lobaa dared to protest her dismissal. She even had the temerity to claim that two of the monks had attacked her, dragging her into the garden potting shed and in turn forcing her against her will. But since the monks were celibate, this was impossible. Lobaa must be a liar as well as a wanton. She was barred from the monastery's environs.

Now, not quite four years later, here she was again, balancing her child, a solemn little boy of three, on her hip.

Worse, she insisted not only that the child was the son of a monk and the grandson of her father, the late Tiktaalik Lobaak; she claimed he was also Lobaak's Embodiment.

This presented the monks with a host of problems. Should she even be permitted to approach the courtyard's interior? What about the child's lack of a father? Should she be allowed to register her claim? If she did succeed in having the child registered, should he be examined? If by remote chance he displayed any of the signs, then what? A blood descendant who was also an Embodiment might establish a hereditary dynasty, not a monastic one.

Although the great brass gongs resonated six times a day throughout the monastery with the summons to meditation, there was little serenity to be found among the monks.

It became so disruptive that Tiktaalik Yimnaamik felt forced to act.

First, he permitted Lobaa and her son to enter the inner courtyard, be registered, and be tested. He reassured the monks that this was merely a gesture necessary to dispel rumors, one he was certain would lead nowhere because Lobaa was obviously an opportunistic trickster.

Next, he announced that only those candidates and families already waiting in the inner courtyard would be tested, and that the outer gates would now be sealed against all other claimants until further notice.

He himself tested Lobaa and her son, and he himself announced the results. The woman and child were charlatans. Who could corroborate her dreams, since there was no husband in her bed? Could not the birthmarks on the child's ankle have been skillfully administered by tattoo? The child's precocity could not be denied: he spoke clearly, with an impressive vocabulary for a three-year-old. But that could have been taught him by his mother, who also likely tutored him on details of his grandfather's life, about which he seemed fluent and which she had known firsthand. As for the fountain of shooting stars that accompanied his birth, every monk who monitored the heavens knew such celestial displays were not uncommon at that time of year, miraculous though they might seem to the uneducated populace.

Lobaa and her son were dismissed and publicly denounced as defilers of devotion.

But Lobaa did not leave.

She protested the finding. She claimed that a lifetime in obedience—first to her father Lobaak, then to him as Tiktaalik, then to the monastery, then to Lobaak's Return as her infant, and now to that Embodiment, her son—was devotion at its essence, beyond possibility of defilement. She claimed that the phenomenon of such devotion could be explained only by the most intense faith; she insisted that lifelong, patient sacrifice sanctified itself. Otherwise, she added—an odd expression clouding her usually impassive face—such patience was inexplicable.

She stood outside the great gates, clasping her son.

As the other claimants were duly processed through testing—and rejection—she returned, day after day, simply standing at the outside gates, holding her child. On their way out, the family of one dismissed candidate passed her, stopped, and watched her for a long time. Then, assuming she must know something they didn't, they joined her, with their own small would-be Tiktaalik in tow. Curious, other families slowly gathered. Nobody asked anyone else what they were waiting for, since everyone presumed the others must know the answer and no one wished to appear stupid. The crowd that had once clamored for admittance now stood silent outside the gates, waiting for no one knew what.

Tiktaalik Yimnaamik watched this mysterious assembly, day after day. He pondered what to do about these plain, stolid people, whose sunburnt, broad-boned faces reminded him of the peasant parents for whom he'd been one too many mouths to feed, who had given him over to monastic life.

Then he had an epiphany.

"What fools we've been!" he muttered to himself. Still,

more than a fortnight passed before he was able to convince the other monks of his plan's soundness.

But finally one morning, as Lobaa and the crowd behind her took up their usual stations in silence, the monastery's exterior gates swung wide.

A procession of monks emerged, bearing baskets laden with rice and grain from monastery storerooms, beakers of oil and beer, vats of cheese, and small purses of coins. As if waking from a trance to realize that this must be what they had been waiting for, the crowd surged forward.

A riot seemed imminent.

But Lobaa, her son astride her hip, stood between the crowd and the monks. She raised her hand. The crowd halted. They respected her, for she had been the first to wait. She called for patience, and assured everyone that she had taken note of who had been waiting longest and thus should be attended to first. She then read names aloud from a crumpled sheet of paper she pulled from her apron pocket—listing herself and her child last, to everyone's shocked, admiring whispers. Thereafter, the goods and coin were distributed in orderly fashion.

The people drifted off, busy with their newfound bounty. Only a few stragglers returned the next day, none the day after. But Lobaa came back each day and stood with her son: an unsatisfied, unspeaking accusation.

At last, Tiktaalik Yimnaamik issued a proclamation. He announced that the monks would draw up more stringent tests for a candidate Embodiment. He acknowledged that true Embodiments presented themselves very rarely, perhaps once in two or three centuries, so that most Tiktaaliks would be openly elected by the monks, after all—but now only after consultation with elders among the people. He conceded that excesses had been made in governance, and he vowed that the monks would take pains not to fall into such error again. He pledged that in future the monastery would have greater respect for the daily needs of the populace.

Busy with their provisions and reassured that more would be forthcoming, the people barely noticed the proclamation.

Only Lobaa still stood, silent, clasping her child, at the gates.

Then, the next morning, she was gone.

Tiktaalik Yimnaamik was greatly relieved.

But as time passed, he was surprised that he could not forget her. Indeed, he found himself as curious about why she had left her post as he had been about why she had taken it up in the first place. He felt oddly responsible for her, which he told himself was absurd. He also felt uneasy. He had not been that certain her child's birthmark was merely a tattoo, not that certain the child had been coached, not that certain he himself had been right in making an example of Lobaa in the face of all the other, blatantly fraudulent candidates. Not at all certain … in growing discomfort, he sent monks in search of her.

But she was not to be found. She and her child had left the district. One midwife reported that mother and son had joined a passing caravan, and that before leaving, Lobaa had confided that in order to remain, she would have been forced to hide the boy—though she didn't say why. No one had any idea where she had gone.

But the townsfolk, on hearing that the monks were seeking her, now began saying that her son had all along struck them as a genuine Embodiment. Some insisted they had known from the moment they saw him, that he wore the air of an entitled Tiktaalik, that his breath smelled of lotus honey and his eyes were old and wise. Others confessed that this had occurred to them while standing with his mother outside the gates, when she had listed herself and her child last though everyone knew they'd been there first. A few admitted it had dawned on them only after the woman and child had left the district.

Eventually, they came to speak of the child as The Lost Tiktaalik.

They began to celebrate the anniversary of the day it was said he had been born. They began to celebrate the anniversary of the day it was said he had vanished. Not knowing what Lobaa had named him, they made up names for him among themselves. They began appealing to him in their thoughts as one who would understand.

Finally they began to worship him. They were certain that his mysterious powers had been proven, in that he was embodied by absence and thus everywhere evident.

As for the monks, they continued pacing and chanting, living and dying to reverberations from the great brass gongs, but with more self-control and compassion, for a while. Given the tighter strictures, few candidate Embodiments presented themselves as Tiktaaliks, and those who did were almost always found unworthy.

Several centuries later, the monastery was compelled to build a golden-spired shrine to The Lost Tiktaalik, so large was his following. Furthermore, a new tale had become a legend throughout the district. It was about a woman who had strange dreams when pregnant. She had given birth—but then had hidden her baby son. It was said he grew secretly into a wondrous child, a true Embodiment—the Embodiment of The Lost Tiktaalik.

By the time a few more centuries had passed, there were no more Returns of any monastic Tiktaaliks. There were, however, numerous Embodiments of The Lost Tiktaalik, whose pagodas were everywhere, and everywhere were filled with devotees and petitioners, including monks busily lighting candles, burning incense, and spinning prayer wheels.

Historians studying the period have written scholarly treatises debating the meaning of this thriving belief. They still argue about whether this was a tale of ultimate revenge by a woman whose patience had been one-too-many-times aggrieved; or the account of an ambitious, cynical wench with a gift for invention; or the story of a simple woman who, having no husband through whom to live, lived through her son as she had through her father; or the legend of a natural leader who arose when there was a need to confront injustice. At least one scholar, fascinated by the narrative, even wondered whether Lobaa might not have been a new kind of saint—one free of any deity, unfettered to any heaven. Against his own scientific beliefs, this scholar found himself wondering whether The Lost Tiktaalik, finally adored as a god throughout the region, had been, in fact, some sort of an Embodiment. But if so, of whom or what?

Nothing was ever proven, of course.

It is possible to prove counterfeits, but never possible to be certain of the real thing.

THE STOOP

The stranger sat, head cocked, listening into the silence that followed the story's end.

"Ah," he said after a while.

The Yarner continued her work, knitting needles ticking steadily in rhythm, a ribbon of softly nubbled wool widening from the waltz of her hands.

"Thank you," he murmured. "That was a story."

"Not a hedgehog, eh?"

This time he hazarded a smile.

They sat that way, unmoving except for the woman's arthritic fingers darting, looping, tugging.

"Why do you really think," the stranger asked into the space between them, "that people need—want to need— gods?"

The Yarner paused, resting her work in her lap. She sighed.

"Beyond the obvious, I mean," he went on, suddenly anxious not to appear naive, "the fear of meaninglessness, the longing to appeal to—bargain with—something more powerful. An answer to their prayers—"

"Nonsense," she snapped. "If people wanted answers, they'd pay more mind to science. People don't want to be answered. People want to be heard."

He sat up, curious.

"Haven't you noticed?" she went on, "Almost everyone would rather have you listen to their story than grant their wish. A stranger is only someone whose story you haven't heard yet; an enemy someone whose story you refuse to hear—or who refuses to hear yours. That's what people really do when they pray: tell their stories. Oh, a reply would be nice, mainly to acknowledge somebody's heard them. But a reply isn't *necessary*. People invent replies, signs, miracles, anyway. Most even regard totally unresponsive silence as proof of their religious belief—though I've never been able to work out proof of what? That something all-powerful is ignoring them? I wouldn't find that comforting." He chuckled. But she added, sadly, "Think of it, all those stories, passionately hurled out into an indifferent universe. Like comets—trailed by a brief arc of fire signaling *Look! I was here! I have been somewhere, meant something, mattered!* At the heart, though, they're still rock, ice, and dust."

"So … in a sense, storytelling is praying?"

The Yarner frowned.

"No. Prayer is storytelling, but not the reverse." She pointed a knitting needle at him for emphasis. "Prayer is storytelling without the discipline, responsibility, skill—without the *listening*—this craft demands."

The stranger flinched at the needle but persisted.

"Listening to what?"

"To the characters, first of all. To the story's listeners, while it's being told. To other yarners—especially those who went before. To oneself, the teller. To silence. *Making*—storytelling, artistry—demands listening. And time."

He felt a confusion of clarities.

"Then aren't you just saying that we all try to invent meaning? Religionists from outside themselves and makers—yarners, musicians, carvers—from inside? Are you saying that those who can't be storytellers settle for prayer?"

The Yarner started gathering up her things.

"Are you hungry?" she asked.

Even more curious now, he nodded.

"Come inside, then," she said, getting to her feet with a small groan and then leading the way, "Everybody says daft things when they're hungry enough. It'll be time for supper soon. I can feed your brain a tale while cooking something to feed your belly."

And she led him into the little house.

THE LIST KEEPER

Once, far from here, there was a mountain village known for its spring splendor of azaleas and laurel. Sometimes City people would travel there for a brief holiday, just to take in the brilliant, fragrant display. But there were no fitting accommodations—only a small, rather primitive inn—so visitors rarely stayed the night, retreating instead to the nearest district center. Since flower-gazing idlers disrupted village work-rhythms, the locals did little to encourage the tourists to remain.

It was a busy village, what with herding the goats upmountain for months at a time, and fishing the river, and tending what crops could be coaxed to grow in the terraced, rocky soil.

No one wanted to be bothered with record keeping, yet everyone knew such drudgery needed to be done for the good of all. Who had planted what and where. How such-and-such got traded from this one to that one. What inheritances did the dying leave and to whom. Who got betrothed or wed, who left whose household taking what with them, who was born, who died. So the village employed a woman—forty or so years alive, though she looked older—as their List Keeper.

She had first appeared as a floral-seeking tourist, but stayed on when the others left. She put up at the inn without complaining about its missing amenities, and she went about noting which species of flower grew where—listing varieties of laurel, charting the crisp reds, sunrise pinks, and flaxy whites of the azaleas—apparently for her own pleasure. No one asked about her life, nor was she forthcoming; she seemed to have little or no attachment to any former existence, which the villagers assumed must have been back in the City. Eventually, impressed by her quiet diligence—and bereft of list-keeping services by the recent death of the elder who'd performed this task—the villagers posed the issue of her becoming their List Keeper. She accepted.

They were surprised. But it was harvest time, so they hired and then promptly forgot her.

As her stipend, the List Keeper was given use of a small hut at the edge of the village, what food she needed, hewn firewood, and candles, ink, pens, and ledgers ordered from the City or acquired from the rare passing caravan. She led a fairly solitary life. The schoolteacher sometimes visited to chat briefly, and the village waif would stop by, eager for any bits of food. But in fact, she remained an outsider, despite having now dwelt in the village for more than a decade. This was due less to any unease the villagers might have felt about her unknown past (had they been sufficiently interested) than to two conflicting factors in the present: she performed what the villagers regarded as menial labor, yet she carried herself as if her work were of the greatest import. To the villagers, it was inconceivable that such devotion could be felt by anyone about creating anything inedible, unwearable, or uninhabitable. Nor did they spend much time reflecting on this. Meanwhile, she held herself apart and the villagers didn't care, so long as she worked hard. Which seemed to suit her.

She dutifully kept track of all items, acts, transactions, pledges, promises, and dates she was supposed to catalog. Unlike her predecessors, she actually expanded the job. For clarity, she added categories, then subcategories, and she kept special calendar notations alerting her when she was supposed to remind who about what. She shelved the many separate ledgers in an orderly fashion, building an archive year by year, each ledger filled with her neat, small, evenly formed letters and numbers, columned side-by-side down each page.

No errors. No crossings out. No blots. A work of beauty.

She also kept a secret ledger, wherein she listed her private thoughts.

One entry read:

A list is a memory fossil.

The first writing ever discovered was a numbering of market goods, an inventory—a list.

Lists inspire specificity. They notate time. Perhaps they create time, because they are sequenced.

Lists bestow deep satisfaction, due to their potential for being checked off. Sometimes they even invite the later addition of already noted items or already accomplished tasks—just for the pleasure of checking them off.

I could stand in one place my whole life, and not be able to list everything around me. I could be rooted in a square waiting for massive gates to pour forth such plentitude of understanding as to make keeping track irrelevant, or I could be drifting in a whirl of river so swift its eddies are unlistable, or I could be listing all the questions I haven't yet thought of, or trying to keep track of all the temptations I have not yet resisted. The lists are there, whether I can find them or not.

People have fought, killed, and died, because of whose name was found in certain lists. Or not found.

Lists are everything. Rational thought. Alphabets. History. Science. Mathematics. Music. Relationships. Recipes. Vows.

All art is comprised of lists and intervals.

My kind—list keepers—we are artists.

It's a shame, really. People ought to give us more credit.

Another of her entries read:

There are list makers and list keepers. They are not necessarily the same.

List makers do not always keep faith with what they've noted down. At their extreme, list makers can order others to do things, assuming that others exist to obey.

List keepers, however, do not always show imagination worthy of interpreting what lists require. At their extreme, list keepers can be content carrying out orders.

Fortunately, I am both a maker and a keeper. I must never take such responsibility lightly.

Another entry read:

Ours is not a quest to acquire or control. We make lists against chaos. To remember, analyze, understand. To share knowledge—even if it is the knowledge of chaos.

Other people keep lists of what needs doing, then do it. For me, keeping lists is The Doing. Anything else is superfluous.

Another entry:

Babies and young children love lists. They know lists help you remember. They know lists are funny. They know lists are singsong playthings.

Old people, as they peel off minor memories, become expert list makers. Snuff out the candle, Bring in the shawl, Keep a list of the places where you might have put your lists. They often make lists of what happened to their lives, so that others won't forget them. Remembering is a social act: I fear being forgotten so long as I myself remember me. But once I no longer can, why would I care what anyone else remembers?

Women keep lists. A lot. If women didn't keep lists, everything would never get started, let alone done.

Young men should keep more lists. It would be better for everyone if they did.

Day in and year out, the List Keeper went her rounds, collecting information, classifying it, cataloging it.

This increasingly demanded that she notice. All the time. It demanded that she notice what was noticeable and what was not always noticeable. She could not help noticing, in fact. Noticing had become her way of being.

But in order to notice what required listing, she also had to notice what didn't.

She had to notice what starts before, exists outside of, spills over from, borders next to, and follows after whatever gets judged list-worthy.

Of these discards, she found herself making lists.

She noticed she was doing this despite awareness of its being a hopeless task. But it felt intensely important, recognizing those unaccounted-for acts, acknowledging those discarded realities—like sweeping a courtyard that would merely get dust- and dirt-streaked again. Or washing a bowl merely to fill it with food again merely for the food to be eaten merely again to wash the bowl.

Trying to make lists of the discards made her realize how truly rare an Only is.

So she began to make a list of Onlys.

Because it was a short list, it took more time to compile than a long one.

Even so, every entry (the uniqueness of each snowflake, for instance) wound up sharing so much commonality (a snowfall, for example) that she wasn't at all certain what could accurately be defined as an Only.

Indeed, if Onlyness was a characteristic every Only had in common with every other Only, then how could it truly be an Only? She worked well into the night, falling asleep over her ledger.

The next day, she realized that it all came down to choice. It came down to the judgment of what and how to list whatever and however, since she—since no one of her kind—could possibly list everything anyway. This realization about choice temporarily paralyzed her thoughts. But the habit of discipline was so strong in her that she began listing the variant ways she might choose to exercise such choice.

She wrote in her private ledger:

I have been listing the wrong things! Shovels and coins, linen lengths, acreage, debts and payments, people's opinions. That's absurd! I have been scribbling my lists off at the edges and corners, while major occurrences are eternally happening at the center! I should be listing Eternals! I should be listing stars in the firmament, breaths inhaled and exhaled in a moment, an hour, a single day. Dreams—I should be listing dreams! Shadows! Hiccups! Types of laughter! I should be listing the Unlistable ... I should—

She never finished that entry.

This was because the third day, while pondering Eternals, she fell into the dizzying insight that each Eternal she could manage to notice, would—*if* noticed closely—fade toward its own time in which to vanish. This epiphany ricocheted her back against the ultimate victory of chaos.

The List Keeper began to shiver.

As an act of will to calm her trembling hands—she hated erasures and wouldn't tolerate blots—she started listing the multitudinous ways in which chaos inevitably erodes order.

Then she had a staggering revelation. She wrote in her private ledger:

> *There are no Eternals.*
> *Or else Eternals are not eternal.*
> *They don't exist. At least not eternally.*
> *Only chaos might be eternal.*
> *But that would be a kind of order.*
> *I suspect that even an order of chaos is denied us.*
> *But who would do the denying? To posit denial at all is to impose purpose and blind oneself to chaos.*
> *Yet if there are no Eternals—except possibly chaos—it means the only items that lists can ever record are endless categories of ending, of burning away, of dying.*

She stopped, pen in mid-air.

Her hand began to shake violently.

But she forced herself. She wrote. Slowly. Deliberately.

> *All I really do is keep track of loss.*

She burst into sobs.

She keened. She mourned and rocked herself, overwhelmed by cumulative, incalculable loss; devastated by loss, mourning all the items on all the lists that could not be listed and all the items on all the lists that could be listed but to no purpose except the exercise of listing them. A mountain wind sprang up and bore the sound of her lament up high, away from the village. No one heard her.

It was more than a week, in fact, for the villagers to notice her absence. Two neighbors fell to blows quarreling over who had borrowed whose grappling hook. One herder had forgotten the date he'd put the rams in with the ewes for tupping, and a farmer couldn't recall which paddock he had planned to leave fallow for hay. The village sage, also its vintner and its drunk—Old Uncle, as he'd been called by generations who'd never learned his name—had perished in a blissful stupor, and been given a rowdy though unregistered funeral. Everyone was waiting for their collective memory's custodian to tally, record, check, change, or consult something, waiting for the appearance of their List Keeper on her usual rounds to collect information or requests for it, to offer answers, to remind them of whatever it was they needed to remember.

They waited despite a growing discomfort that no one had noticed or could recollect when her visits took place. But it didn't matter much, because they were certain those visits had been consistent and reliable, although admittedly not always welcome, because she could be so picky about exactitude, so willing to correct approximations. Still, it turned out that she did possess a strong memory, to which she could commit many details—which meant that often she could answer questions on the spot during her rounds, without having to consult the archived ledgers. This capacity, resulting in the speed and convenience of an immediate response, was much appreciated by the villagers, and even when her professional recollections differed from their own, they chose to respect hers, assuming hers were validated by the ledgers. Shrewd in their simplicity, they also knew that a village lacking records was fertile for the growth of misunderstandings and broken promises, for arguments smoldering into fights that flared into feuds—confusion at best, enmity at worst.

Yet now, when they asked after her, no one had seen her.

Finally, the village council decided someone must look in on their List Keeper. The affable midwife was everyone's choice.

But when that old woman knocked at the door, there was no answer. Gently, she nudged it open—the village scorned locks—and spied a whirlwind of objects scattered on the floor before her: pens, crusted pools of dried ink, torn leaves of paper, overturned cups, a comb, kicked-off slippers … then, raising her lamp and peering into the darkness, she saw a figure hunched in a corner, moaning.

"My poor child," she exclaimed, shuffling toward the huddled shape, "What happ—"

She stopped in her tracks as the List Keeper raised her head.

That face was a dazzle of pain, tear- and ink-streaked, swollen by grief. Weeping had rinsed all brightness from those eyes.

"*Rhododendrus ponticum five-petaled! Tupping time candles two ounces newborn!*" the List Keeper whispered urgently, tugging at the old woman's sleeve with ink-splashed fingers, "Who pastures betrothed musical notes not nothing? Additup! Choices oh how end where begin catalog dogmatism wise child slain rain pain cannot *oh oh ohhh*!" She broke out sobbing.

"Wait, wait, my dear, I cannot understand you," murmured the old woman. She reached toward the List Keeper's despair, but the younger woman's arms were flailing so wildly that her visitor stepped back, wincing.

Yet the List Keeper went on babbling through her tears.

"Stopped too soon everything never gets started yet ends end endings? *How have I where have I lost it* the list of the lists of everything lost—"

"Child! You *must* calm down. How did—"

"*It's a wedding it's a bedding it's a breath it's a death*," the List Keeper sang, "Oh oh," she implored, "*Want* to be calm not care not *notice* fuchsia future rapture rupture Who knew this said that? sold it stole it hid it fed it? hated loved it hurt it killed it? No ink no matter mutter blood marks keep track *cannot* keep track lost track *loss* ..."

Finally she subsided, whimpering with exhaustion, and allowed the old woman to enfold her. They sat that way a long time.

The villagers met and discussed what was to be done.

It was obvious that the stricken List Keeper would require time to regain her senses—if she ever did. The midwife argued that the List Keeper had now quieted down and seemed almost content, sitting day-long outside her little cabin, watching with close attention how a particular tuft of grasses grew there. Certainly she did no harm. But other villagers maintained that she no longer performed the task she had been hired for, so why should they feed, house, and support her to watch grass grow? No, they needed to find and engage someone else to do the clerkish, irritatingly necessary labor of list keeping, since their From-the-City List Keeper (which is how they now derisively referred to her) had gone mad with her own inflated importance—or else was simply too lazy to do her job.

The villagers were in no way a cruel people, but they found this dramatic situation disorienting. Thanks to her self-indulgent collapse, they complained to one another, the whole village was suffering. Quarrels spread and deepened—over promises broken, over possessions, over differing interpretations of paddock-fencing measures, even over the wording of Old Uncle's axioms, his sole legacy. With no List Keeper to consult, suppressed animosities surfaced, while fresh antagonisms took root. At last, the near-murder of one villager by a neighbor over land boundaries served as a sobering crisis. The villagers needed to employ a new List Keeper—swiftly.

But that could not be done without first formally disengaging the one they already had. No one knew why this tradition was observed, though some thought it was plain practicality: to protect the village from having to support more than one hired person at a time. Still, it seemed a decent enough rule. Besides, the elders said it had always been done this way, and the village had enough problems without breaking precedent as well.

So what was to be done with her? Really, she should not have to be their responsibility. It was not fair. After all, she had interjected herself into their lives, had imposed herself on them when they happened to need a List Keeper. She should be shipped back to the City, though they had no idea where to in the City, or indeed if she had come from there in the first place.

The old women's advice prevailed. The midwife knew of a healer in a neighboring district who had over years built a haven for the sick, the mad, and the needy. The community welcomed everyone, though mostly women and children wound up there.

That was where the List Keeper would be sent.

And so she was, accompanied by the midwife who, on her return, reported that her charge had gone peaceably, chattering of tulips and turnips, laughing quietly or singing to herself, counting her footsteps as she walked. What later became of her the residents of the village never knew.

But since she wasn't there to remind them, they soon forgot to wonder about it.

THE KITCHEN

They were sitting at the scarred oak table with one tippy leg, the remains of supper before them. The stranger sopped up the last spicy smear in his soup bowl with a chunk of bread, downed it, and exhaled, closing his eyes in contentment. He could barely remember when last he had eaten so fully or so well. Four helpings, he thought, and her not minding a bit.

The Yarner studied him. Then she rose, cleared the bowls and spoons, and put out a knife and a small wooden slab, followed by a wedge of yellow cheese and a basket of fat purple grapes—"From the vine in back," she said. He'd pushed back his chair to rise and help, but she waved him off. "Later, perhaps. If you learn where things belong." Then she brought two pottery cups, and poured some wine from a jug into each of them—"Same vine."

The wine was surprising: soft and complex—its taste as mellow as its color, like an heirloom ruby. The stranger could feel his muscles begin to unknot in its warmth.

They had munched peacefully through dinner. He had the

35

impression that his host did not value chatter. Also, it must be admitted, he was slightly afraid of her. In the absence of conversation, her last story about the List Keeper remained sharp-edged in his mind. Perhaps that had been her intention.

"In this world," he ventured at last, picking up a thread of their unspoken dialogue, "the sane person is at a disadvantage."

The Yarner sniffed and cut herself a slice of cheese.

"That why you laughed?"

He looked puzzled.

"I meant no disrespect—"

"Took none. But you laughed."

"I thought parts were funny," he said, a touch defensively, "though painful. When she was going mad. Or … going sane, depending."

"Glad you laughed. That story is meant for laughter."

"Because it's funny that the sane person—in this case the List Keeper—is at a disadvantage in this world?"

She cocked her head. "Depends what advantage is. Not many risk doing work they love, no matter the cost. "

"Torturers can love their work."

"True. Thank you. I was being imprecise. I should have said, 'Not many risk doing work they love—work worthy of love—no matter the cost.'"

"Because the cost is always greater than one expects?"

"Not necessarily greater. Different."

"Perhaps those who don't risk it have no choice," he mumbled.

"Mmm. So we all say. But it's also true that most people settle for labor. Some can't conceive of any other option. Others resign themselves to what they've been told: that work by definition is the opposite of pleasure. That's a thought so commonly shared it appears safe, so they come to call it sanity. Eventually, they believe it." She shrugged. "Still, what's tragedy to some is comedy to those who know how to enjoy it."

"Enjoy what?"

"Tragedy, of course."

He wanted another cup of wine, but was reluctant to seem greedy. Unasked, she refilled his cup and her own.

"Before you took up this work," she asked, not specifying what she meant by that, "did you ever settle for labor?"

The stranger's expression hardened. He sipped his wine. Finally, he said, "I worked for some years in a pit, mining salt."

"Salt."

"In parts of the world, you know, salt is costlier than gold."

"Oh yes," she said softly. "You can cure with it, preserve with it, eat it."

He wasn't listening. His body was tightening with recollection.

"Some of us cut the salt and some of us hauled it. Straining to push or pull or carry those blocks of salt uphill from the pit …" He fell silent.

"Uphill from the pit …" she coaxed.

"From the pit." He spit out the words. He was finished. He gulped some wine.

She picked up her knitting and began tugging a knot of yarn free of its tangle.

He didn't speak. And then he did. But so softly she leaned in to hear.

"Every day, glistening in the sun, all you could see was salt. It hurt your eyes. Everything bleached out and became salt. Every night, you smelled salt. Day and night, you tasted the grains lodged in your teeth. You breathed salt. You inhaled the particles, then retched them back up, gagging salt. Salt crumbs crunched beneath your feet, gouged your flesh when you fell, chafed into your cuts, stung your scars livid again. Salt crystals furred your skin. Salt possessed you. You were owned by it, heaving it up on your back, straining under it uphill bent almost double beneath the block's weight; your stare focused only on the path in front of you, watching for your feet watching one foot then the other appear and disappear in and out of view in and out; blinking the salt sweat out of your eyes; watching those feet move you and your burden slowly toward release at the summit. Where some days you could feel a breeze. Where you could lay down the salt block. Where you could rest … But only for a moment. Because you had to descend into the pit again and do it over again, and again, and … between such days and such nights, you did whatever you could—lied, stole, fought, hurt someone, chugged cheap grog to sleep free of dreaming—whatever it took to feel alive. To survive. But you didn't survive. Every escape was imaginary. Each route your brain devised was only inspired by a bad dream the night before. You're still there, you'll always be there. The only reality is salt. The only action is strain."

"It was not a good way of being alive," the Yarner whispered.

"It is not a good way of being alive," the stranger said.

"It is done. You believed you had no choice."

"I had no choice."

"Certain of that."

"Yes." His answer was clipped. "Since then, I've worked at many kinds of labor to earn my bread. Sometimes I've taught music. Mostly I live as a street musician. I'm poor, but my time's my own. I've never again mined salt." Then he added, "How few do you think are aware they have options?"

"Too many to risk them."

"Yes."

"Yet you are here."

"Yes."

"And you never stopped living, even in that tenth circle of hell."

"No."

"And you never stopped listening for stories."

"No."

"I've sometimes wondered," the woman suggested, "if thinking about doing something isn't more exhausting than doing it."

He said nothing. He was remembering how a wound can become everything, the whole world, and how once a wound becomes the whole world, the only choice is to agonize over it or earn a bitter pleasure from it, even if just by not looking away. I chose the latter, he thought. Some people mistake acceptance as resignation.

"Perhaps," she murmured, "we discover the true limits of the possible only by inching, fear after fear, just a few, maybe a few more, stumbles, past those limits. Into the—"

"—impossible."

Whether with that word he was confirming or disagreeing apparently mattered less to her than his having completed the sentence. She stood up.

"Time to sleep," she announced, clearing the cups, fruit pits, and cheese rinds. "Your room is off to the right, just there," she said, pointing toward an archway. You'll find towels, fresh linen, and quilts in the room. Also clean clothes that ought to fit you—left by a previous traveler. Have yourself a good wash, and don't feel you need to stint on hot water. It may look rustic here, but we live in the Trust's greatest city, after all," she snorted, adding wryly, "We enjoy modern amenities, though mostly the simplest ones. Sleep as long as you need. You should find everything you require. If not, tell me. But in the morning. Get through the night yourself."

He rose and bowed slightly, the formal courtesy belying his appearance.

"Thank you for your kindness. And for the stories."

She peered at him again.

"Another yarn later on then. Perhaps tomorrow. Or … after you settle in." She bustled toward a hallway to the left of the kitchen.

He sat down again, suddenly exhausted. "Discovering the limits of the possible," he muttered to himself once alone, "with hindsight—easy enough to say." He looked around the kitchen, taking in each simple utensil in its neat place. "But *before*, while seeming wears the power of being …" he whispered in awe, "then the impossible is a wonder that can never be understood."

From the dark hall her voice floated back.

"If a wonder is not a wonder once understood, it was never a wonder at all. Dream well."

THE CHILD WHO COULD READ RIVERS

Long ago, in the days when truths and gods were plural, it was the old women who spread the news. Wherever they met: at the stream for laundry or the well for hauling; in each other's kitchens, shelling peas or putting up preserves; around each other's hearths, quilting; wherever they gathered to work, they talked. For them, words and work were inseparable, and since they were almost never idle, they were almost always talking.

Of course the fathermen and the young people dismissed it as gossip. But they listened eagerly enough whenever the old women felt disposed to share information, and they grew nervous when the women shuttered their eyes and wouldn't speak. Everyone knew that no matter what anyone called it, revelation or rumor, it was crucial to survival.

There was a deliberate morality to this process. Too sophisticated to believe in objectivity, the old women acknowledged their biases, yet trusted each other's different partialities to maintain balance. They did not pass along to the general community news that was untrue or unproven, lacking in insight, merely cruel, or leading to no solutions. This was how the old women had developed and refined a system of ethical governance in a mode forged to feel ageless, organic, and invisible. It was how they constructed, nurtured, and enforced the social order. Without their ancient form of intimate communication—usually nicknamed for food: dish, juice, morsels, tidbits—other information, however presented, tasted superficial: bland data lacking context and the nuanced seasonings of analysis, mercy, or judgment.

This was long before people would come to forget that a human mind, repeatedly assaulted by torrents of unconnected details, begins to lack the desire for using such information, especially to affect change, particularly profound change, which the old women sought subtly to inspire. They did so by their one art: the virtuosity with which they practiced gossip.

So naturally it was the old women who were the first to notice, then verify among themselves, then spread the news.

The child Daki could read The River.

The River had no name. Its name was The River, just as the villagers called themselves The People. Village life, health, economy, communication, mobility—everything vital to The People—depended on The River.

Naturally, over millennia, this reliance had fostered periodic experiments, as generations of villagers studied whether or not, and if so, how, to influence the creative and destructive powers of The River—to placate it, perhaps even domesticate it.

One such experiment had been to worship The River, bargaining for favors with gifts of sacrifice and flatteries of supplication. Another had been to dam it up, another to divert it, another to shore up the banks.

But given sufficient time, rocks dislodged by the rapids

gouged and destroyed every dam. The flow refused to follow diversions. The current overbrimmed every reinforced bank. At whim, it seemed, The River dropped its level to near-dry sand-bed, or it mysteriously muddied and thickened. And it seemed to flood when it wished, heavy rains or not. Yet all the experiments, over time, worked. Until they failed.

But, argued the fathermen, there was no way to be certain about one experiment: the effect of worship. Perhaps the floods *might* have been worse, or The River *might* have dried up more often, or *might* have drowned more incautious victims in its rapids, without the ritual offerings cast into its depths. So did the nonresponse of their deity elicit in many villagers—who formed a group calling itself the Followers—the inspiration to continue, even intensify, their worship.

This one experiment was thus retained, and in time it was becoming part of The People the people were becoming.

Nevertheless, despite or because of this belief, some villagers never surrendered arguing that there must be a way to fathom The River so as to harness its powers. The Fathomers were smaller in number than their religious neighbors, but no less devoted to their own pursuits. Moreover, each of what became two factions had its own internal schisms.

The Followers were ceremoniously observant, but split into numerous sects and sub-sects, ranging from those who believed The River was a god and must be prayed and sacrificed to, through those who believed The River was a metaphor for god yet should be prayed to for the exercise of faith, to those who weren't sure The River was anything but a river—yet considered it wise to worship on the safe side of things.

Meanwhile, the other, nonreligious faction, the Fathomers, scornfully rejected a safe side of anywhere. Yet they, too, splintered, though only into two sub-factions: those who believed The River was not a god but mused that it might be somehow sacred and longed to grasp what that meant; and those who felt The River was neither a god nor sacred but who wanted to understand what The River *was*.

The two major factions had begun their dialogue amiably enough, since they shared the goal of understanding The River.

But once the Followers gained more adherents on the safer, thus more popular, side of things, they had a revelation: they realized that a majority could not possibly be wrong. Earlier, they had proselytized the Fathomers from concern for the latter's welfare; now they did so from their own zeal. When this pressure met with resistance, they began to view the Fathomers as a threat to their hegemony, and so denounced them. Faith, not proof, was the point. They had once regarded the search for proof as benign, in itself a type of faith in the existence of proof, however elusive. Now they rejected proof as destructive.

The Fathomers, first irked at being proselytized, then offended at being pressured, and finally infuriated at being denounced, felt besieged. Grievance and besiegement, combined with smaller numbers, can inflate self-righteousness from a comfort to a certainty. So the Fathomers announced that proof negated any need for faith. They had once regarded faith as harmless enough, sometimes even useful during the long, difficult search for proof. Now they rejected faith as destructive.

Soon the Followers accused the Fathomers of being arrogant, aggressive, and condescending in believing themselves abler to decipher great mysteries. The Fathomers accused the Followers of being ignorant, uncurious, and superstitious in their insistence that mysteries were unknowable. After generations of this, the factions rarely spoke except in acrimony. They feared and detested each other so heartily that their differences, not The River, had become the subject.

In the end, the only thing that united all sects of both factions across mutual loathing was the search for how to control the power of The River. Yet this unifying motive was no longer acknowledged by anyone.

And now suddenly, it seemed, the child Daki could read The River.

The old women said so.

If the news hadn't come from that source, no one would have believed it, for at least three reasons.

First, who could read rivers? The Grand Fatherman alone dared scry The River's moods, and then only in abstractions describing what, according to the Fathomers' scorn, everyone already knew: "The Waters are troubled today," he would interpret gravely before performing the sacrifice of a lamb, offered in placation to the roiling current.

Second, the villagers were a plain people. It had been only twelve centuries since they had learned to read words on parchment, and only ten since they possessed their own codices, mostly for recording trade. A few villagers exchanged letters downriver with relatives or friends who had left for the valley or journeyed so far as the City. Visitors rarely passed through. There was little time, given the demands of farming, fishing, and herding, to read for any reason other than practical utility, so reading was not held in particularly high esteem. They employed a woman to handle the lowly tasks of tracking trade records, chronicling births, marriages, deaths, and the like.

Third, Daki was an unlikely savior, one who couldn't even read words, much less rivers: a strange, silent child, orphaned by The River, shunted from one household to another. Separate, swift, rainstorm risings had claimed Daki's father while he fished and then mother while she scrubbed clothes on the bankside rocks. Daki had no sisters or brothers, and had no friends. Children felt uncomfortable around someone they thought simple in the head. Cruel ones laughed. Kinder ones smiled vaguely and hurried off. Already eight years alive, Daki went unschooled, and had to be supervised when pressed into helping out at harvest or shearing. But since no one seemed much concerned, the orphan also ran a bit wild, disappearing for days, sometimes glimpsed wandering alone by the riverbank. Certainly no one thought any child, especially this one, capable of succeeding where Fathomers, including young, strong sonmen, and what Followers, including mature, sage fathermen, had failed.

Still, the old women said so. The child Daki could read The River.

This information, once circulated, was considered sufficiently urgent to convene a special village meeting—the result of which, after much solemn discussion, was to send to the City for a Grammarian.

The Grammarian was quite young, and understandably proud, as she was the first woman to hold that post. She sent word back that she could hardly be expected to travel to a remote village to solve some impossible riddle about an urchin claiming to read rivers, since she was busy with important matters. This was less than completely true: she was at that moment learning how to fire clay in her pottery class, a hobby she felt strongly she deserved. The young Grammarian, aglow with her fresh triumph as an historic personage in the profession of her father and uncle, had begun to realize that the long-coveted post, for which she had labored so ambitiously, required that she "waste" herself, as she complained, largely on tasks she did not wish to perform.

Nevertheless, after the villagers beseeched her again and again, she relented and made the journey, traveling through the summer heat in a rosy haze of martyrdom—an attitude that helped prepare her for the moment when she was shown her accommodations at the tiny inn. The Grammarian was audibly unimpressed. Nevertheless, she called for the child to be brought to her for interviewing—a meeting that would have to be brief, since she must return to the City the next morning.

So Daki was brought to her and stood sullenly staring at the inquisitor's feet, which were shod in elegant boots of soft crimson leather. The villagers backed away and left the two alone.

Two hours later, Daki burst out of the inn scowling, and ran off along one of the riverside routes to solitude. The village elders assembled in haste to await the Grammarian's emergence. When she appeared, she did not invite them inside but addressed them from where she stood, framed in the narrow doorway, fanning herself with a silk kerchief. Not knowing what else to do, the villagers squatted or sat down on the ground, where those in the front row found themselves staring at the crimson boots.

"Well," she began, clearing her throat. "It was difficult to get the child to talk. But I succeeded." She flashed them a self-congratulatory smile. "I have my ways." The villagers applauded politely. She nodded in acceptance and continued, speaking with the excessive certitude employed by persons unsure of their subject.

"It's all nonsense, of course. And ridiculously primitive. The child claims the riverbed is composed of both subject and object—which is to say theme, argument, thesis, substance, text. The rocks in the rapids are nouns. The current is tense— past, present, future. Everything is both subjunctive and indicative, which is absurd. Flotsam and foam are adjectives."

The villagers gaped.

"The child just describes. He didn't give these things their proper grammatical names, of course. *I* did that."

The villagers stared.

"Oh," she trilled a short laugh that seemed to emanate from some internal bubble of genuine humor, "and the fish are verbs. That's quite delightful."

There was an embarrassing silence. Every villager was concentrating hard to comprehend … well, any of it.

Then the Grand Fatherman stumbled to his feet.

"But," he began tentatively, "what does all that *mean*? What is The River's *message*?"

The Grammarian looked shocked and a little affronted. She seemed to rock back on her little red heels.

"You," she replied coolly, "fail to understand who I am. I am the *Grammarian*."

People stole glances at each other. Somebody coughed.

But the young Grammarian was a woman of self discipline. She managed to transcend her impatience and to smile with a façade of studied tenderness—a face one might aim at small children incapable of grasping complexities one was stooping to teach them.

"I am the *Grammarian*," she repeated, more loudly, as if they hadn't heard her. "I didn't ask about *meaning*."

Then she announced that she must retire, since she would leave early in the morning to return to the City.

And so she did.

But not before shutting the door to her small, bare room, where she sat down on the hard cot, kicked off the red boots, and thoroughly soaked her silk kerchief with tears of sadness—for herself, for the crazy waif, for these ignorant peasants, for the whole unbearably poignant world. The young Grammarian frequently suffered such emotional fragility of late, since she was living with the desolation of having got her wish.

For the villagers, however, life provided no such desolation, and her departure seemed to end the inquiry.

It was getting on to autumn when, during the quarterly season-meet, the old women again raised the issue that the child Daki could read The River. This time the reminder was met with some irritation from both Fathomers and Followers, as it was generally thought rude to raise a problem if no one knew how to solve it. Besides, by now both Followers and Fathomers were comfortable in their settled enmity. The old women, apparently, were not.

Then the schoolmaster spoke up.

He was a mild man, and shy. He had stuttered as a child, but persevered until now he was schoolmaster, cheerfully offering education to people free from much interest in it. He had grown accustomed to their indifference to, even rejection of, learning for its own sake. They tolerated his odd habit—he loved to lie out and study the starry nightsky, even in cold weather—but if a fact or idea wasn't related to crops or herds, he could rarely convince them to encourage their children to study it.

Perhaps in this opportunity he saw a chance to redeem himself in their eyes. Or perhaps it was merely his own curiosity, which, though cramped by his circumstances, remained eager. In any event, he offered to try to get Daki to share whatever meaning the child read from The River.

That the local schoolmaster might succeed at what the City Grammarian had failed (or declined to pursue) was the source of merriment. But since the schoolmaster good-naturedly chuckled along with the rest of the villagers, and since no other options were available, and since the old women, after all, had said …

The villagers decided there was no harm in letting him try.

So the schoolmaster set off to find Daki. Meanwhile, his neighbors turned their attention to serious matters. It was shearing time.

When he returned almost a month later, the schoolmaster came alone. He said he had left Daki living upriver in a little hut he had helped the child assemble from branches, twigs, stones, and sod. Daki already knew how to gather food— edible roots and herbs—from years of forest wandering and, the schoolmaster added, smiling, "This child knows how to catch, cook, and eat verbs."

Some of the old women expressed concern about the child's welfare, living away from the village. But the school-master assured them that Daki loved the hut and that he himself would look in on the child regularly. No one else cared. A few villagers even muttered that seeing less of the weird orphan around the village would be a relief.

But when the schoolmaster began to relate what he had actually learned from the child, his listeners' mood changed.

"Daki says, " he told them, "that The River doesn't 'mean'. It doesn't … signify."

"Doesn't mean … signify … *what?*" demanded a farmer.

"Anything. At all."

"But—what does it *want* from us?" a herder asked.

"It wants nothing from us. No devotion. No sacrifice. It calls out to us not at all. But," he went on slowly, "the child says we must learn to read it nevertheless, listen to it. All of us." The schoolmaster wanted to add that he knew this was a paradox. But then he'd have to explain what a paradox was. Besides, he had to contend with a rising growl from his audience.

But what does that *mean?*

What's the point of listening to The River if it's not calling to us?

This is what you have to tell us? After spending all that time with the mad child?

The schoolmaster grasped his sole fact and clung to it.

"Daki did say one other thing, as I was leaving. Something is happening to the north. It—d-does things to The River that s-sadden the w-waters, or slow or thicken them, or h-harm the fish. It—"

But he had lost his listeners' attention. Crestfallen, he watched them drift away, certain Followers pointedly letting him overhear their disgust. A few Fathomers, faithful to their mission of trying to understand whatever they could, nevertheless announced they would send a group of three upriver to investigate what the northern villages and towns could be doing to The River.

A few days went by. Tempers seemed to calm. Everyone including the schoolmaster returned to reassuringly familiar duties.

Except for certain sect leaders of the Followers. These fathermen, despite their ongoing competition for devotees, united in vocal outrage at the schoolmaster's message. This outrage they expressed generously to their neighbors.

One morning, Daki, wandering through the village as in the old days, was greeted with taunts and a rain of pebbles, and quickly ran off. Hearing the commotion, the schoolteacher rushed out, yelling at the attackers, a gang of Followers' sonmen. Then he turned to follow and comfort the fleeing child. But at that moment, the three Fathomers were sighted returning from upriver, waving and shouting that they had news.

They did indeed. Four different northern villages were making changes to The River. One village had built a seasonal dam. One had constructed a water wheel to irrigate their fields. One drained their marshy bogs into The River each autumn, so they could gather and dry peat for winter fuel. And one had taken to burying their dead on the banks, to ensure that the souls would be borne out to sea.

None of these actions were new to the villagers, since at different times in their own history they had practiced them all. What astonished the Fathomer delegation was the revelation that if these same actions were taken upriver, it *affected* those downriver. Even after some upriver activities ceased, the effect might *persist* downriver.

The villagers were The People, so this had not occurred to them.

They knew other villages along The River existed, of course. They traded with them, despite knowing themselves superior. But this news—the concept of durable, intimate connectivity—disrupted their sense of what was real and shattered their assurance of centrality. Worse, in such unsought but unavoidable connectivity, they could not only be affected by others, but by inferior others.

Meetings were held, arguments shouted. Many Followers declared that nothing could affect The River except supplication and sacrifice, adding that the Fathomers, as apostates, doubtless invented this news from the north. Many Fathomers contended the Followers were being willfully blind to clear evidence. People stalked out of meetings. But the old women insisted they return, and finally a sufficient number of individuals on both sides reasoned their way through to a compromise.

Another delegation was chosen, this time from both sides, as emissaries to the northern villages. They were to bring gifts and initiate discussions about how villagers living along

The River might work together, so that none would suffer from actions taken by others.

This process—lengthy, arduous, and over the following centuries incrementally successful in cooperation and alternately lethal in belligerence—is its own story.

That is not this story.

This story is about just how outraged the Followers turned out to be.

For one thing, where would all this end? What if there were villages further north along The River? How to know what they were doing? Must The People explore the whole world? And what time did that leave for farming and fishing and herding, and wouldn't their way of life be destroyed and wouldn't they then all starve and perish?

For another thing, the newfound interdependence between villages meant this village was perhaps not unique. That meant that The People could claim no special intimacy, or even history, with The River. Its villagers might not even be—preposterous thought—the only ones who were The People.

But the worst offense was rooted in the schoolteacher's original report:

Daki said The River cared nothing for devotion and sacrifice. Daki said The River called out to The People not at all. The River was indifferent.

This was insupportable. It left nothingness. A dry abyss of despair.

Still, just how outraged some of the Followers were only became known after the schoolteacher went to look in on Daki's hut a few days later. It was late afternoon when he returned.

His screams preceded him. He could be heard from a mile off, crying out.

"Sh-Sh-Shame! Shame! *Sh-Shame!*"

People rushed from their homes to gather in clusters, all chatter hushing as he approached.

As he drew nearer, they could see that he was staggering, lurching, as if from grief to grief.

He was carrying something they could almost make out. It was a form, not large, limbs dangling: an unweaned animal, a lamb or a kid.

"*Shame!*" the schoolteacher screamed, his voice cracking, his face a red blubber of tears and spittle. "*H-horror.*" He stumbled toward a leader of the Followers.

"*S-st-stones,*" the schoolteacher hissed, "*You* know … H-hut. *Ashes* now. B-b-b- …" He licked his cracked lips and tried again, spitting each syllable out with effort. "*Burnt. Hut. Ashes* … ev-everywhere ashes b-b-blood! And y-your s-*stones*!" The Follower stepped back, glance cast down. The crowd pressed closer.

Then they saw.

It was neither a lamb nor a kid. It was a bundle of rags.

No. It was—he was carrying a child.

It was the broken body of a child, small bony brown legs dangling, twig-like arms crooked unnaturally, blood clotted on the little head lolling against the schoolteacher's shoulder.

"N-n-never harmed a one of us. B-burned and s-s-stoned … left for d-dead. Who *are* we, *animals*, that we *d-do* this?" The schoolteacher began to howl, a lost animal himself.

Two of the old women who were healers rushed forward to lift Daki from the schoolmaster's arms.

"I d-don't think—" he cried, "I'm af-fraid—"

But the child's eyes fluttered open, and Daki murmured in a soft high voice, "Don't need. To *mean*. Just *is*. Anybody can—see … just look—"

"Yes, yes!" the old healers almost sang, "here, give us, give us the child! We can heal, we know ways—"

But Daki murmured again in that sweet small voice, "No secret, just *is*—ever'body knows ... down dee ..." then smiled and died.

The sun was cowering low in the sky by the time the old women had finished bathing the bloody face, washing the broken body, winding it in their best spun linen.

A few Fathomers built a raft, placed the child on it, and bore it solemnly down to the banks Daki had loved. A few Followers, moved by this act of reverence and a vague sense of collective guilt, walked beside them. Together they waded in, floating the raft out into waters that had claimed the orphan's mother and father, and would also claim the raft and its small burden as part of what now would be read as The River's meaning.

The vessel and its occupant swept rapidly along the current from past through present to a future unknowable as the great open sea, riding waters that ran clear of flotsam and foam. Only a few fish, silver darts of energy streaking in the sunlight, accompanied the raft until it was borne out of sight.

For three days and three nights the wailing of the old women never stopped.

They had never meant to evoke such meaning.

They had not meant to evoke meaning at all.

They had meant for The River's ageless, awful silence to be heard.

But they had failed to estimate what that might provoke. They had failed to gauge The People's vulnerability to three afflictions not all their healing arts could yet cure: the solace of ignorance, the versatility of fear, the satisfaction of cruelty. They had failed to imagine that such disorders might exact a fresh ritual of sacrifice, in which meaning was necessary and possible but inflicted through suffering—precisely the conclusion their subtle means of gossip had meant to prove wrong.

But a few of the people, at least, had grasped the river's silence. This, the old women assured each other, they had at least achieved.

In times to come, the people would celebrate triumphs, abide setbacks, and exaggerate, then forget, both. But the old women did not forget. They never made that mistake again. This was easy enough, since, being old, they had few years to live. What was hard was that younger villagers usually didn't believe them when they spoke of it.

Not that it made a difference, ultimately. When we gaze up into the dark vastness sequined with stars we grow serene, knowing we gain perspective, seeing reality the way it is.

Yet what we gaze at is the past, the way reality was long before we could perceive it.

THE STEPS

"I hadn't—expected that."

"Death?"

"I just—I thought the child would live. I thought the old women would heal him." He buried his head in his hands.

"Old women sometimes make mistakes. We can't do everything. As it is, we do quite a lot."

"You do, you do. Only … I thought … an innocent child …"

"Children are not necessarily more innocent than adults, and almost never as ignorant. Also, having a reputation for innocence doesn't save children from being hurt, as you've doubtless noticed. I warned you. Not all my stories have happy endings."

"Not *all*—?" He lifted his head and looked at her, eyebrows raised.

"You have a point." She didn't smile. "Perhaps not any. Perhaps, in my universe, irony passes for light-heartedness. I admit it: There are places in me—lakes of acid spewing toxic fumes. There are people in me who kill and joy in it, or kill and grieve at it, but kill nonetheless, which may be worse. I'm the world in which the inhabitants of my yarns live. Beware. It's a harrowing place, sour, jagged—though not lacking laughter. If that's too painful, you can always end a story at some different stage—say, when Lobaa is allowed to have her child tested. Or when the List Keeper first settles efficiently into her job. Or when Daki and the schoolmaster build the child's forest hut."

"What would be the point of that?"

"I agree. But they're all perfectly acceptable conclusions. Required ones, in fact, if there are to be happy endings."

"But I don't want happy endings if they're incomplete."

"All endings are incomplete. Any happy ending—if you let it continue on long enough—will turn tragic."

"That's a cheerful thought."

"It is, actually. Because if you let it persist still further, it eventually turns uproarious."

They sat quietly again for a while, each on a different step. They had settled on the stoop again. The afternoon summer breeze was pleasant, sun splashing into warm pools of light between a dapple of clouds and leaves. In one such pool on the step next to the Yarner, her black-spotted ginger cat curled in a sublime doze like a miniature leopard—chin resting on paw, tail-tip shading closed eyes. In counterpoint to the steady ticking of the knitting needles, a jay screeched from a branch of the pear tree, ruffling his azure splendor in hope that some passing female might find him irresistible.

It had been … what? Weeks since she'd told him the story of Daki. Yet this was the first time they had talked about it. Not that he hadn't hinted at wanting to discuss it, but she would not be rushed. Nor was it any use pressing her for more yarns than she was ready to tell before she felt ready to tell them, and to his dismay that readiness seemed to come not so frequently. It was as if she let each story lay down its own spoor, to be followed gradually, however long that took. She seemed confident that he would track a story's trail, and stay to absorb it, however long that took, too.

Whenever he mentioned that the two weeks his rent had purchased were more than up, she waved a dismissive hand. Yet she clearly was not wealthy. She herself had mentioned that few people wanted stories any more, so he wondered how she survived. Then he realized that the nervous, ferret-eyed man who had on two occasions visited briefly, who had inspected and then gathered up her finished knitting and left a purse of coins in its place, was the marketer for her goods. Her beautifully knitted mufflers and vests and shawls, even the potholders and trivets, bought her the time and the freedom to knit stories. As soon as he understood this, he began disappearing every few days for an afternoon during which, until shooed away by the authorities, he could be found at a busy City intersection, fiddling away at the doola'h. Then he could bring back coins, which he placed, mutely, on the kitchen table—and which, with only a nod and smile, she gathered up and put away.

By now, the days disclosed a rhythm.

Mornings were for baking bread, tidying the house and, some days, doing the wash. Mornings were for tending the vegetable, herb, and flower gardens, which had meant planting bulbs in autumn, when he'd arrived; then digging turnips, potatoes, and parsnips in winter. Once the earth warmed into summer, mornings were busy with weeding and picking what was ripe and needed eating. But from the moment spring had trickled in and spilled itself across the garden, mornings were for studying the flowers, to pluck something of beauty—one stalk of ivory milkweed perhaps—

for the house's sole vase: a fragile crystal flute on the hearth mantle. (Her visitor had not yet found the courage to ask the Yarner where this piece—wildly out of place amid the hand-thrown gentian-blue pottery and fire-blackened pots—had come from.) Mornings were also for silence—while kneading dough, sweeping, scrubbing, weeding. The stranger suspected this was so that his host, while she worked, could let her mind range free to find new stories.

Mornings, the Yarner made clear, were for earning mostly leisurely afternoons and serene evenings, when he might strum a melody on the doola'h. Or they might read, silently or aloud to each other. Or they might talk about life and the world's spasms.

She questioned him at length about his having been so engaged in the struggles of the world. He poured out to her his anguish at the suffering he had witnessed, his helplessness about the ineffectiveness of acts he had taken to staunch that suffering, his bitterness about engaging a world so calloused it could forget what only seconds earlier it had witnessed bleeding, and the legacy of guilt he bore at having finally disengaged himself from that fight. She said little.

He once asked her how many yarns she knew.

"I've no idea. Hundreds. Thousands, maybe."

"Then please, why won't you tell me more tales?"

"Because the tales I tell you are meant for you. The others …" she shrugged.

So he had tried to learn to wait. Sometimes he felt a twinge of resentment. How could she deny her yarns to someone who had journeyed this far to find her? Who was she saving them for? What was the use of being a yarner if you didn't share yarns? He was hungry for tales, greedy for tales, he wanted scores of tales. And she was withholding them from him. He tried to push down the irritation and learn patience. But some nights, lying in bed, he could not fathom why he stayed on.

Yet when he drifted, for lack of the yarns, to joining in her daily rhythms, it felt as if they had lain in wait within him all along.

How long *had* it been? Time felt unreal. No, that wasn't true. Time felt real enough, just unimportant. He had joined in the rhythms of the house, and also in its simple and, he found, satisfying chores.

He accompanied the Yarner on those afternoons when she ambled to a neighborhood market, returning with her basket filled with cheese, a fish, some fruit, a few eggs. Since there apparently had not been anyone younger, taller, and stronger than the Yarner in the house for a while, there was also quite a bit of lifting and reaching to do, including returning volumes to their places on high shelves of the library that spilled into every room—at least into each of the few rooms he'd been in, though he knew that the house had other rooms, further along the central hall, into which she sometimes disappeared for hours at a time and about which she never spoke.

He wondered about those rooms, inventing furnishings, even inhabitants, although he never heard sounds emanate from them.

But the library was enchantment. Merely touching books thrilled him. To hold the words in your hands, turn a delicate page with a sensuous gesture of the wrist, as if unwrapping a mysterious package. Indeed, sometimes a dried flower—a ghostly violet, a rose—was pressed there. To smell that faint perfume! To caress the paper leaves pulped from rags or wood—some pages nubbly as raw silk, some smooth as petals, each texture a feast for the skin to graze. The different formats and sizes: large as small tabletops, or able to fit in the palm of one hand. The range: from reference works thick with thousands of membrane-thin pages, to slender volumes of poetry. Sometimes the bindings, sewn webs of fibers frayed with age, linted under his breath. And the colors! Threads yellow as sulphur, or in a glory of vermilion, or cobalt blue; the page tones varying from chalk-white through pearl to a shade of ash alien as a meteorite. Sometimes the inside covers had endpapers with designs that shimmered like heat waves. Sometimes the pages were edged in gold. The books were a host of yarners standing in wait for him. Day after week after month, through winter evenings, sometimes whole nights, he read—poems, science, stories, history. Merely tidying the books or fixing a warped shelf felt comforting.

In fact, given his memories of mining salt, he laughed at the mildness of his current labor: sweeping the hearth and laying fresh fires, sifting the garden compost bin; rolling up the worn rug, hauling it outdoors, and thrashing it until such clouds of dust rose that the Yarner came out to ask him what offense the carpet had committed. Soon he found things to do on his own—fixing the wobbly table, oiling squeaks in most of the house's hinges, repairing a loose rocking-chair rung, sanding splinters in the front stoop steps—the very steps where he and the Yarner now sat in the late afternoon sun. At the beginning, he had sensed a subtle, proprietary resistance to his inserting himself in his host's familiar rounds, so he had become careful always to ask permission before embarking on a self-chosen task. But she too had changed. Now she'd say, "Do as you like. Do what interests you."

He suspected she was glad of his help. He also knew she was irritated about her difficulty in performing these tasks herself—due, she had once sighed to him, to the way her joints were succumbing to age. He suspected, in fact, that she was in more daily pain than she ever let on—from pride?

vanity? fear of losing control and independence? He knew enough not to ask. So he proceeded with his tasks, some of which people might call 'women's work', and others of which they might term 'men's work', but he didn't stop to notice the difference.

"Wait ..." the stranger said. Something about *the difference* brought him back to thinking about the story of Daki. "Wait."

The Yarner paused, squinting down at him from her step.

He was thinking why he was thinking what he was thinking. His brow furrowed with it. Then he had it.

"Oh, yes! In the last story ... Did I ... miss something?"

"Probably," she chuckled.

"Was Daki—was Daki a boy or a girl?" he asked.

The Yarner got to her feet, warding off the hand he extended to help. She stood, hands on her hips, glaring mildly at her guest.

"You're not going to be one of those now, are you?"

"One of whose?"

"Why do you need to know?"

"Whether Daki was a girl or a boy? Well, because ... because you must have mentioned it and I must have missed it."

"I didn't mention it so you didn't miss it. Until now. Nor am I going to tell you now."

"Oh. It was on purpose, then. Because it matters."

"On purpose, yes. Because it doesn't matter. How would knowing change the story for you? What difference would it make?"

"I don't know. Maybe no difference. I'd have to think the story through both ways to grasp how each version appears."

"Appearances can deceive while being grasped. For instance, I am a comely young woman, and I find you ... shabbily attractive." He thought she snickered, though whether in malice or mischief he wasn't sure. She was also deft at changing the subject.

"But … When I first arrived? You said yourself that you were an old woman." He was trying not to sound rude.

"No," she snapped, "That is not what I said. My precise words were *'When you look at me, you see an old woman'*. I even warned you *'Do not be deceived'*."

"So you did." He shook his head sheepishly. "So then, what should I do? Is there a—a *way* I should listen? So as to pay closer—"

"Though it may be physically possible to listen and talk at the same time, it's rare. And I think you an unlikely candidate for such an undesirable accomplishment, anyway."

A spasm of pain rippled across his face. Her words could cut.

"You are. A Yarner," he said, each word costing him. "You know who you are."

"That hasn't always been the case. There're still plenty of days I'm not at all sure."

"I don't think I believe that. But in any case, I—I … don't know if I am. A Yarner. A maker of—and meanwhile, I am too old to be a sonman, but neither am I a fatherman."

"Sadly, more lads would do well not becoming the men their fathers were."

"I know I'm not a Follower. A Fathomer, perhaps, since I want to comprehend—what, I don't know. Anything." He held out his hands, palms up, empty. "I look at others, men especially, and I never … fit."

"We might all do better if more lads didn't fit with other men."

"I understand Lobaa," he persisted, uncomforted, "because I understand waiting. I understand the List Keeper, because I can grasp loss. And I understand the schoolteacher's curiosity,

64

his courage, and certainly his despair. But I fail to understand what my part is in … anything. In *this*. I've been here how long? It's already summer. I don't know what I'm doing here."

"Then stop. Stop waiting. Stop forcing your way into what welcomes you. Stop trying to possess what you already own."

Her ball of wool had been sent bouncing toward the tree-pit, and the cat, wakened by human movement and ever hopeful this was a sign of impending food, spotted rolling yarn. The coral-tongued yawn and inverted U of the feline stretch were preamble to imminent coil-and-leap. The Yarner glanced at ball and cat, but she was too slow and the stranger was there before her, fetching the yarn and placing it in her hands.

"Daki's was a dark tale," he mumbled, "That's all I meant."

"I know," she answered gently, smoothing the yarn. "Thank you."

"I … wasn't prepared."

"Yes."

"I thought I was."

"Don't we all think that." She slid her knitting down the needles and put them in the basket. "Well, don't fret. I'll go in and start supper. Bread, cheese, cold sorrel soup I think, yes? Potatoes fried with onions. Wine. Maybe some conversation. Maybe you'll play some music. Maybe the ease of silence. … That's about as pleasant a day's ending as life offers, were we to savor it."

He looked up at her. In the flicker of sunlight he could after all almost see the younger woman she—was? was once? was still?

"Sit out as long as you like. Supper won't be ready for a while," she smiled, "And I know just the yarn to spin you next. Whenever next comes."

THE HANDMAIDEN OF THE HOLY MAN

Once there was a man thought to be holy. He sat near the top of a mountain. He sat there night and day, and it seemed that he never moved.

Some said that he was always praying, or that he meditated, or that he saw visions.

Some said that this must make him holy, or at least wise.

No one could quite recall when he had first come to sit on his ledge in the mountain. But almost everyone could remember that at one time, years earlier, pilgrims had made their way up to him, not without difficulty, to put before him their disputes, their spiritual questions, their despair, their own attempts at holiness.

His judgments were so severe, however, and were delivered in tones so sternly contemptuous of the seekers, that the same visitors rarely returned—and in time, as word spread, fewer and fewer pilgrims wound their way up the narrow mountain path. At last, only one or two a year would approach the holy man, and then as if he were an oddity, a curious sight to be stared at, not a living saint to be questioned or followed, hearkened to or imitated, or even perhaps wholly trusted.

Finally, almost no one came at all.

He still sat, nonetheless, on his ledge, seeming to gaze out over the near and distant peaks of other mountains, his eyes blinking now and then against the wind, his flesh wasting away toward desiccation—his body a bony triangle of spine balanced on a base of crossed legs, a gaunt skull at the apex. He seemed never to speak, though his lips could be seen moving. No one could possibly estimate his age.

All this time, you understand, the woman known as the handmaiden of the holy man remained faithful.

It was the handmaiden of the holy man who built the rickety lean-to that sheltered the holy man's body from the rainy season. It was she who had guided visitors up the strenuous path in the old days, and she who still could be seen sometimes scouring the valley villages as if to recruit new pilgrims. It was she, of course, who begged for his food, and carried it up to him each evening in the wooden bowl that was known throughout all the villages as 'the holy man's bowl'—this despite the fact that no one could remember ever having seen the holy man carry it.

But then, no one could recall ever having known the woman's name, either, although she was familiar to everyone in the area. Indeed, she might never have had a name of her own. She had become, in any event, simply 'the handmaiden of the holy man'. And although two or three villagers might whisper in dispute as to whether the mountain's recluse was holy at all, and although one or two villagers might even wonder at the definition of the begging bowl as the holy man's when he had never been seen carrying it, no one seemed to question the title of the woman known as 'the handmaiden of the holy man'.

Perhaps this was because she had announced herself as such so fiercely and for so long that no one cared to argue the point—though no one could actually recall when, or if, she had begun giving this impression. Or perhaps this was because no one else was eager to compete for either her title or her task—and while ignoring a holy man's teachings wasn't that uncommon, letting one starve to death would have brought shame on all the surrounding villages. Perhaps, too, the title 'handmaiden of the holy man' was simply an accurate description of what appeared to be her life.

What else, after all, was she?

Year after year, the handmaiden of the holy man was assailed by questions.

In the early days, the questions had come from outside herself. But as the pilgrims stopped approaching and, later, as even the reliable donors to the bowl she bore stopped inquiring about him, the questions began from within herself.

It was not, after all, as though she had a right to be surprised. He had made it clear from the beginning that he was fit only to be a holy man. He had made it clear that he must sit—withdrawn from all material, fleeting, menial concerns—purely himself, focused on his thoughts, on a mountain top. If the world came and asked anything of him, as had pilgrims seeking counsel, or if the world came and offered anything to him, as had contributors to a beggar's bowl, that was the business of the world, not his concern. Neither compassion nor gratitude must distract him. Even though he had never spoken this aloud in words, the empty spaces socketed behind his eyes had told her so. The handmaiden of the holy man could not say that he had ever deceived her.

Yet year after year she was assailed by questions.

She remembered that in the early days, the questions pilgrims asked her had seemed at first impossibly difficult to answer.

They asked, "What is the holy man really like?"

They asked, "Can he work miracles?"

One or two even asked, "What's it like—to be the handmaiden of the holy man?"

She recalled, with a wistful smile, how her replies had changed over the years.

In the beginning, she had maintained an enigmatic silence while wearing an expression that intimated she knew far more than she would ever tell. Later, hard pressed and feeling sympathy for the questioners, she had begun to invent answers. Sometimes the answers would vary from pilgrim to pilgrim—which the villagers interpreted as further weighty mysteries of contradiction. Thus she added to the legend of the holy man, when actually she was merely experimenting with various responses to see which was most effective in hiding her ignorance. This solution had lasted until pilgrims began to ask different questions:

"Why is he so severe in his counsel to us?"

"Why does no mercy temper his judgments?"

"Do we interrupt his meditations or his mission?"

Only then did the handmaiden of the holy man begin to reply simply, "I don't know."

At first, this response felt to her like a shameful admission of her own ignorance. In time, it felt to her like a betrayal of the holy man. At last, she grew indifferent to its being anything but the truth.

Now she told herself that eventually the questions that assailed her from within would grow as irrelevant as those from without had become, even though these new questions seemed far more difficult to respond to than any of the world's curiosity.

"How did I come to be here?" the handmaiden of the holy man asked herself. "Did I choose this freely? Have I spent my life, serving him, to no purpose? Or am I using him as an instrument of *my* freedom, while believing myself an instrument of *his*? Did he ever really need me to serve him?"

These and many other questions the handmaiden of the holy man asked herself. And she found that she could invent answers to all of them, as she had done at one time with the questions of the pilgrims. As before, she found that she often had different answers to the same question, and that these answers gave rise to still more questions. She was dazed by these questions. They preyed upon her constantly. Even asleep in a nest she had built for herself one ledge down from the holy man's lean-to, she dreamed more questions. By day, treading her rounds in the villages, she moved as if groping her way forward inside a private swarm of questions—so much so that she began to forget to recruit pilgrims.

Some villagers assumed she was in a mystical state of transcendence contracted from having lived for so many years in close proximity to a holy man. Others thought she had gone deaf or lost her wits. Yet they had no reason to fear her even in this new state, so they averted their gaze from the absence in her eyes, contributed to the holy man's bowl she carried still, and let be.

She was waiting for the third stage: the one where she would simply be able to say "I don't know" to all the questions, and be free of them. It had happened before. Why shouldn't it happen again?

Another year passed. And another.

Still the handmaiden plodded her rounds, waiting.

But now her questions grew to obsess her, for she was weary of invented answers, unable to find real ones, and still incapable of embracing her ignorance.

One day, more exhausted than her completed rounds would warrant, she bore the bowl—how it seemed to get heavier each year!—up the winding path to where the holy man sat on his ledge, strands of his long hair lifting in the wind, his lips moving slowly.

She had been in five villages that day, and had walked for miles, yet no more than usual. Vaguely, she recalled something—what was it?—through the babble of questions in her mind:

Is he a holy man?

Who am I to question?

How can I cease to question and be at peace?

She recalled that the villagers had seemed especially kind and patient with her that day, and the thought occurred to her that given their generosity and the heaviness of the bowl, the holy man would have a special feast tonight. Not that he cared for such matters, as he was above lowly things. The handmaiden of the holy man knelt to set the bowl at the holy man's feet.

It was then she saw to her shock that the bowl was empty.

At the same moment, she knew this was not because the good villagers had refused to fill it.

All at once, her questions parted like a veil and she glimpsed the reason the bowl was empty—as filled with terror at this apparition, and as awed, as one who spies the naked face of a god.

The handmaiden of the holy man had that day forgotten to beg.

She rose from her kneeling position. She faced the holy man, who stared not at her but at the distant mountain peaks. She stood, while the wind whirled around them both.

She began to ask him her questions.

As if in a dream, yet more awake than she had ever felt herself before, she heard her voice quietly pose question after question, pulling each one out of herself trailing anguish and laying it, like an offering, at his feet.

The lips of the holy man ceased moving.

It seemed to her as if the two of them had been poised that way for eternity, winds whipping around them, her questions falling one by one like fireflowers into the abyss of his silence, her eyes fixed on him, his eyes fixed on the distance.

Then she had no more questions.

Yet still she waited.

It seemed to the handmaiden of the holy man that she had lived and died a thousand thousand lives while waiting for his answer to reach her through his silence.

But no answer came.

She bent again, and gently pushed the begging bowl she had borne but which everyone seemed to know was his, closer to him, in a tender gesture that seemed to say he would have need of it now. She noticed one drop of water making a glistening rivulet down the sloped wooden side of the bowl, to lie like an eye or a diamond at its center.

Then she realized, astonished, that it was a tear, and that she was weeping.

She stood again, and peered off into the distance toward which he stared. Her whole being followed her gaze as she strained to glimpse what he saw.

But there were only the far-off mists ringing the snowy peaks.

The handmaiden of the holy man turned once more to look at him, and through her tears she smiled a forgiveness more infinite than she had known she possessed.

Then she turned and walked slowly down the winding mountain path.

The villagers were surprised to see the handmaiden of the holy man descend the mountain path in the evening, accustomed as they were to her visits earlier in the day. They watched as she moved through the villages, and a few wondered if the glint of moisture on her face could possibly be tears. But they decided it must be the evening mist, for she had never been seen to weep.

She walked faster and faster, and her face seemed almost a blur in the blue light of dusk. Each village she passed through assumed she was journeying to some destination in the next, and it was a few days before everyone in the surrounding countryside came to understand that she had stopped nowhere. The handmaiden of the holy man had disappeared.

Everyone's first concern was for the holy man, of course.

Since he had not come down to beg with his bowl, he must be starving up on the mountain ledge. A delegation of villagers was hurriedly assembled from candidates whose self-righteousness was fortunately greater than their reluctance. They labored up the steep path, burdened by baskets of food and a sense of outrage that the handmaiden of the holy man should have deserted her post, necessitating their having to perform this direct act of charity themselves.

They told one another that the handmaiden was an ingrate who had betrayed her master as well as those whose generosity had enabled her, for years, to bring him a laden bowl.

They told one another that she was a fool who had never been able to appreciate the holy man's teachings the way they themselves had.

They told one another that she was a doomed soul fallen into wickedness, for obviously she had sought the pleasures of the world in turning from the liberating path of sacrificial service to which they themselves had never aspired.

They told one another that she was a madwoman, for who else would brave the world alone after such a sheltered existence? If she somehow managed to escape death, more degrading ends would await her. One or two members of the delegation did wonder what could have driven her away. But so durable was the tradition of veneration for a holy man—even a holy man not visited in years—so durable was the tradition of veneration for the *idea* of a holy man, that those few who found themselves momentarily curious about the handmaiden's motives quickly suppressed such heretical thoughts.

As the delegation of villagers neared the top of the mountain, however, their chattering chilled to a hush. Each one was remembering what little knowledge they all, any of them, actually had of the holy man.

Those who had made pilgrimages to him years earlier recalled the severity of his judgments, the distance in his voice, the way he never looked at his supplicant but fixed his eyes, instead, on the neighboring mountain peaks. Those who had never been in his presence before remembered all the stories they had heard of pilgrims who returned from the holy man's ledge filled with self-contempt for their own hopeless ways, their grossness, stupidity, lack of vision— how such returned pilgrims would sit for weeks in front of their huts, staring into space as their teacher had done, until gradually they realized that others still moved about, lived, laughed, made love, shared food around the cookfires. Then they would discover the greater insight that these neighbors were as hopeless, gross, stupid, and impoverished in vision as they themselves, but lacked their enlightenment in having learned that. And so the returned pilgrims experienced the miracle of a contempt for others greater than the one they had been taught to feel for themselves. And the exporting of this contempt gave them the energy to begin living again, to laugh, make love, share food around the cookfires, and in time forget everything—except that they did not wish to journey up the mountain path again.

Eventually, back and leg muscles straining and nerves in a state of ominous excitement, the villagers rounded the final turn of the path, to see the ledge before them. Shreds of cloth bindings from the lean-to fluttered in the light morning wind, like a lonely, many-armed god beckoning his followers.

But there was no holy man.

There was no one at all.

Only a begging bowl was left, sitting empty on the ledge like a sign, a rune, a signature that a handmaiden had been there; a message that once, someone had given and someone had taken, someone had begged and someone had not, someone had fed and someone had been nourished—and all that remained was emptiness.

For a time, the villagers could talk of little else but the absence of the holy man. After the first delegation returned, carrying their offerings back down with them, other groups wound their way up the mountain path—some to see for themselves, some on the assumption that the holy man would eventually return to his ledge. Indeed, in the weeks following the news of the holy man's vanishing, more pilgrims climbed the mountain in search of him than had ever done when he was there.

But always they found only the frayed shelter in its progress toward gradual collapse, the stark rocks, sparse vegetation, and empty begging bowl. Finally, even this last vanished—into the cloak folds of someone irked that a perfectly serviceable bowl was going unused.

After a while, the villagers reconciled themselves to the certainty that the holy man was no more. Some said he was dead. Some said he had never existed. After all, no one had seen him for years. The only proof they had of his presence was the perpetual, taken-for-granted existence of his handmaiden, at least until she had suddenly left him—or left them.

And where they initially blamed her for his disappearance, they came to blame her for his existence, for having invented him in the first place, as an excuse to beg for unearned sustenance, because everyone knew that she herself could never have been holy.

In this manner the villagers comfortably solved their disturbing mystery, and their lives went on as before.

But then, strange rumors began to drift among them about the woman they had for so long called the handmaiden of the holy man. These were rumors that she had been seen again— but each time in differing circumstances.

A group of village women who had journeyed to bring their handicrafts to the district market said they saw her telling fortunes by the cards and spinning yarns in a stall at the marketplace. The yarner's name, one had learned, was Ankha.

Another woman, returning from a visit to her mother in a distant village, sent word back to her sister that the handmaiden of the holy man was a well-known figure there, going by the name Meilade—a healer who had founded a haven for the sick, the mad, and the needy, though mostly women and children wound up there.

A husband and wife, gone out from the foothills to the plains to trade with an expected caravan, had both seen the handmaiden of the holy man—though they quarreled over the details. The husband remembered her riding in a palanquin, adorned in the finest scarlet silk, reclining against cloth-of-gold cushions; he had inquired of a caravan traveler and learned that the lady was Bretiang, a courtesan renowned for her wit and beauty. His wife, however, insisting loudly that all women looked alike to her husband, said that *she* had *really* seen the handmaiden of the holy man, but certainly not as a courtesan. The wife saw her wearing a man's loose trousers and wool cloak, riding at the head of the caravan on a fine stallion with a coat the shade and sheen of midnight satin; she said the handmaiden had been calling orders to a group of followers who addressed her respectfully by the name of Oon.

Two young men, libertines from a particularly rowdy village, swore that while out hunting they were attacked by a wild woman of the woods, who hellishly yowled, "This from me! This from Uxten!" with each blow she dealt; she was, they said, easily recognizable as the handmaiden of the holy man.

A small child who wandered away from home, following the trail of bright orange field daisies with dark velvet centers that grew along the foothills, returned home safely the next day. When questioned by his frantic parents as to how he had survived, the child answered that the lady who used to beg with the bowl took care of him and set him on the path toward home. The lady's name, as the child pronounced it in a babyish lisp, sounded like Evaraze.

For years, different folk from surrounding villages claimed sightings of the woman once called the handmaiden of the holy man. Always she appeared in new circumstances, and always with a different name. Yet in all this time, no one had seen even a shadow of the holy man. Nor had anyone, for longer than the villagers now cared to remember, climbed the mountain to look for him. They were as certain he was dead or never had been there at all as they were convinced that his handmaiden was alive, and everywhere.

One day a stranger passed through the villages in the valley.

He moved slowly, staggering, leaning heavily on a staff. No one knew him, but he seemed old and fragile, and given the traditions of the valley, he was invited to share food and shelter at a house in each of the villages through which he passed. People felt touched by his humility, his gratitude for the crumbs they offered.

When questioned, he replied only that he was a wanderer who had traveled much in search of a great treasure he had lost, yet had never really owned. Mystified by this answer, the villagers shrugged and left him his secrets. A few might have pressed him further, but something in his manner—like the echo of a chord struck in mourning—restrained them.

With considerable effort, he shuffled on, as if toward a destination. Not all the concerned remonstrances of pitying villagers, not all their generous offers for him to remain with them—for after all how long could such a frail old man last?—nothing could detain him. He came finally to the village nestled at the foot of the mountain and rested the night there, again welcomed as strangers should be welcomed.

Yet when dawn broke, the children of that house, rising early to peep at the visitor, found him gone. They ran to tell their parents, who thought it strange, but shrugged sleepily before yawning into their morning chores.

It wasn't until the sun was well up in the sky and people were bustling about their daily tasks that someone happened to glance up and shout to the others, "Look! Halfway up the old mountain path! It's the stranger!"

Indeed, far up the slope, his back as twisted as the path, the stranger could be seen, wending his way up the mountain as if he were being driven by a force stronger than his feeble body could contain.

Alarmed for the old man—who must have lost his senses, his way, or both—some villagers dropped what they were doing and ran toward the mountain path. But he was too far above them for their shouts to reach his hearing. So a small group began to climb after him, some of its members irritated at this interruption of their routine and others grateful for it. They were certain they could overtake him quickly, for they were hardy people in the fullness of life and he was a barely fleshed skeleton. But with each turn of the path he was further ahead of them than before, and soon they realized that they might have to climb all the way to the top before reaching him.

And so they did.

But when the villagers breathlessly stumbled toward their destination and rounded the last curve of the path before the highest mountain ledge, they stopped, dazed, at the sight that awaited them.

Not one, but two old people sat on the outcropping, talking quietly.

Just behind them, a bit farther back in the overgrowth, stood a small cabin, its thatched roof spreading shade from the intense sunlight over what looked to be a little garden that put forth rows of vegetables and flowers in jaunty defiance of the stony mountain soil.

The villagers stared in amazement, glancing back and forth from garden to hut to the two elders deep in conversation. Then, perhaps because the surroundings provoked a dim recognition, the village midwife spoke up.

"It's the handmaiden!" she gasped. "The handmaiden of … and him, he's the holy man!"

The stranger turned from his conversation to the villagers, showing them a face blasted by awe.

"I am only a poor stranger here," he cried, "But this"—he gestured toward his venerable companion—"is a holy woman."

A low laugh spun itself out from the woman, a laugh strong and nubbly as the wool of a mountain sheep, a laugh that wrapped them all, stranger and villagers alike, in the safety of its warm folds.

"No, no, my friends," she said, shaking her head in

disappointment but still laughing an irrepressible music to the words she almost sang. "The time for that is past, if ever it had a time at all. We are each as holy as we dare comprehend ourselves to be."

The eyes in the old woman's wrinkled face glowed, her gaze probing each villager's soul as thoroughly as the sun reaching into the rocky crevices of the mountain.

"You see?" she went on, in a voice as excited as that of a child presenting a gift labored on by hand for a long time, "There is nowhere any of us are *not* holy." She turned to the old man.

"We must tell them what we've learned," she said.

The villagers drew nearer, but cautiously. Nestled at the old woman's feet was a snow leopard, its dozing huffs thrumming a background rhythm to the story unfolding before them.

"I wanted to be free of the world," the old man began softly, "so to escape it, I came up here, long ago. But my freedom lay all in the keeping of another's labor. I had not asked for this, but I accepted it. I saw no other way to be free of the world. And"—the stranger bowed his head—"I came to hate the one on whom I thought my freedom depended."

Then the old woman spoke.

"I wanted to be free of others' ideas of freedom," she smiled, "and I thought to accomplish this by giving myself … away. But never having had myself, I had nothing to give. In time I wanted one thing only: to be free"—she turned to the old man—"of your freedom. For this, it was necessary that I conjure myself."

And so she had gone, the villagers learned, down into the heart of the world, to conjure herself.

And so he had gone after her, the villagers learned, in search this time not of his freedom but of the one who had stolen his freedom from him.

But everywhere the holy man sought his handmaiden he found only someone with a name of her own, and he found only himself, and he found only the world.

Homeless, he saw those rooted to one place.

Possessing no goods, he saw those bound to their possessions.

Drifting at will from village to town to city, he saw the faces of those staring fixedly through prison bars.

Lacking family of blood or choice, he saw those who live and die with people to whom they cling from fear or loneliness, lust or habit, calling it love.

Ageing, he saw the young trapped in impatience, the mature enslaved by immediacies, the old shackled with regrets.

He learned that no living thing was free—and this bitter knowledge released him from his search for freedom and for the one who had taken freedom from him. It also unspooled in him a thread of connection between himself and everyone in this shared predicament—whether they knew it was a predicament and was shared or not.

At last he decided to return to the mountain ledge—expecting nothing and no one to await him or recognize him—there to die in the place where he first lost the freedom that had never been his.

All this time, the woman who had been called the handmaiden of the holy man had gone in search of the self she was conjuring, the self beyond the self who would be free of the idea of freedom.

Everywhere she went in the world, she saw others engaged in the same search.

She saw a pair of condemned men being marched to their execution in chains, stretching their faces up into a spring rain.

She saw a young girl wasted with disease array herself in finery like a bride, to meet her death with a passion beyond relief.

She saw two women being buried under a blizzard of stones because their love was judged unacceptable to others—and saw how the concern of each woman was to protect the other's beloved body.

She saw a lost child hug itself with delight at recognizing the way home.

She saw a famous hero shudder with fear in his bed the night before a battle—and the night after.

She saw a group of peasants advance on a palace, armed only with ragged dignity. She heard them whisper *"Freedom"* as guards cut them down.

And in all these selves she was at home, and all these selves were at home in her.

So at long last she decided to return to the mountain ledge, expecting no one to have waited and certain no one would recognize her, to live quietly, self-sufficient and begging of no one, until her death—there, in the place she had thought to escape the idea of freedom, to conjure herself.

She had built the little shack from rocks and branches.

She had dug the little garden, planting it with seeds collected from her travels.

She had welcomed the wild creatures of the place, unafraid, until they grew unafraid of her.

She waited for no one, having found herself.

She sought nothing, having invented the idea of freedom.

Then, one day, an old man had come laboring up the steep mountain path …

The light had begun to fade when the villagers withdrew down the mountain. As they descended, they gazed at one another as if seeing each others' faces for the first time.

Above them on the ledge, the two old ones still had much to say to one another, but alone.

Not long after, the man they had once called the holy man died quietly in the arms of the woman they now called the holy woman. They buried him, at the woman's direction, near the ledge, facing out toward the distant mountain peaks.

For another season or so, the woman they had once called his handmaiden lived on in her cabin. There she tended her garden, scolding the snow leopard when he nibbled the petals of her flowers.

Children would often run up the mountain path now, to sit with her while she told them stories and made them laugh and let them play with the leopard—who loved to have his silken stomach rubbed by one child in particular. The children could never get enough of her stories, especially those about freedom—which they kept to themselves, not sharing with their parents, for fear of being misunderstood. But in their later lives, they passed along the tales to their own children.

Once she pointed to a field daisy in the garden, and asked each of them in turn, "Which part of the flower is most pure flower: the dark velvet heart? the orange petals? which orange petal? the leaves? which leaf? the stem? which part of the stem?"

The children studied the daisy. They thought hard, their little foreheads knotted with concentration. But when no one could reply, she would ask them if the flower wasn't in fact all the parts together as one whole.

"Yes, *yes*!" they would yell, jumping up and down.

"Ah but," she would continue, "doesn't the whole flower also exist in each one of its parts?"

The little brows would furrow again.

"Well, if you find an orange petal floating along a current of air on a summer day, what does it bring to mind?"

The children would clamor to answer that it brought to mind a field daisy.

"Just so!" the old woman would exclaim. "The *idea* of the entire flower exists in even one petal, as perfectly as a song hangs in the air after the last note is stilled. That," she would smile, "is something like the idea of freedom. It lives nowhere and everywhere at the same time. It lives in the connections."

The villagers did not always understand the old woman, but they loved her. The children understood and loved her.

When she was found, one bright noon, sleeping peacefully through a night from which she would not wake, they buried her in the garden she loved, apart but not far from the grave of the stranger they had once called the holy man, close to the ledge that looked out over the distant mountain peaks.

For days the children brought flowers to the graves, and for days the snow leopard would not leave the place.

Then one day the beautiful beast circled the old woman's grave three times and loped off across the mountain, leaping to another ledge—where he stopped, looked back once, then turned and was gone forever, vanishing into his wildness.

That was the day the children realized they did not have to return to the mountaintop to tend the two resting places. There was no need.

So they went down again into their homes and villages. There they watched, and thought, and grew, and passed along to others what they had learned.

Far and wide the words spread, until all the people in all the villages in the province knew that they were every one of them a holy being, each a petal or stamen or leaf or stem of an idea of freedom.

And from that province, like the resonance of a song, the idea bloomed into the world.

No one sat on the high mountain ledge any more, and no one ever begged with a wooden bowl. Holy man, handmaiden, stranger, and holy woman—all had gone back into the heart of the flower. No one need take their place, either, as if that place had ever been theirs.

As for the distant mountains, they gazed impassively on the ledge eroding away year by year. And if the mountains had cared, they could have known that what they witnessed held answers to all the drifts of questions that melted, each like a snowflake spoked scarlet and gold in the sunrise, on their ancient and indifferent heights.

THE GARDEN

Lunch had been a picnic—bread, olives, cheese, fruit, cider—
in the garden back of the little house.

The Yarner sat on her favorite lumpy cushion on a stone
bench, knitting, fingers flying at her wool as they usually did
whenever the rest of her sat still, though lately she knitted
more rapidly than at her standard, steady pace. It was a large
piece, much bigger than a shawl, but her boarder couldn't
make out what. Nearby, unfazed by social proprieties, the
ginger cat blithely interrupted its visit by dropping into a doze
while comfortably flattening the parsley patch. The boarder
sprawled on the ground. All three of them were warmed by
the afternoon autumn sun dappling through the old grapevine
that had thickened its gnarls around and between slats of a
rickety overhead lattice.

The man lounged on a patch of grass, long limbs splayed
comfortably, hands linked behind his head as a makeshift
pillow. Then he squinted up at the lattice, wondering if those
broken slats should be his next repair.

He was finally certain that all his bits of work pleased her, because now she always noticed, and always thanked him. But he was surprised at how much the work pleased himself. Yes, the lattice would be next. Once the last grape leaves had yellowed and fallen, it would be easier to find and mend the broken slats. Meanwhile, the drift of a butterfly and soft hum of a bee on nectar rounds added to the reverberations of the cat's purring and conjured drowsiness, so he pulled his cap down over his eyes hoping for a nap. He'd slept fitfully the night before, having dreamed of seeking a teacher only to find a cynical madman who turned out to be himself, a ghostly visitation of the last yarn she'd spun him, weeks ago.

But the sweet autumn afternoon sleepiness wouldn't come. The moment his thoughts freed themselves from practical matters they sped back to larger ones. Hadn't he arrived in autumn? Could almost a year have past? How strange, really, that he was here, in this strange house with this strange woman. How much longer should he—could he—stay? He still knew absurdly little about her, except from what he saw in the way she lived, and in her questions about him, and of course in the few yarns she'd spun. When he could get her to talk at length about yarning, it was almost as good as hearing a new yarn. But he could not get her to talk about herself. Furthermore, he couldn't help but feel that she still was miserly with her stories, as if rationing them. They were, after all, what he had come for. After so many months, his curiosity was becoming more difficult to control, and his resentment at its not being satisfied rose more frequently.

So he pushed his cap back again and opened the dialogue. But cautiously. Abstractly.

"There are quite a few ... older women in your stories."

"Older than what? Don't be afraid to say what you mean. Old. Not old*er*."

"Old women, then. … Why so many?"

"Because at the moment I find myself one of them."

"But you said you weren't—"

"You have to keep up," she said crisply, "Things change. Yarns sometimes reflect conditions affecting a yarner. As if it were possible to bring outsiders in by bringing the inside out."

"So that's the basis for a yarn?"

"Well, hardly the only basis. That would be too crammed with its yarner. In any event, one reason you think my yarns are overrun with old women—"

"I did *not* say—"

"—I know you didn't." She laughed. "You're getting stronger. Good! You were a mangle of a man when you arrived. As I was saying, one reason you notice these masses, these *hordes* of old women"—she raised a hand to ward off his protest, smiling—"might be that not many people, including old women, are accustomed to hearing about old women. Or really seeing us. Not that old men have it easy, either. But they get to be sages and, if powerful when young, sometimes they get to retain power. But old women? We get confused with the background a lot. Most yarns these days get so pinched by their yarners we're allowed only into the corners, you know, as wicked witches or kind, crinkly grandmothers, not vivid main characters. So when you run across a few old women in a yarn here or there, it can strike you as a pushy multitude trying to take over everything."

He burst out laughing at the image of old women descending in hordes on the world. Nevertheless, that mental picture struck him as oddly reassuring, and he felt shamefaced, as he often did when she chided him. But this time he felt flattered, too. He was almost completely at ease around her now, less in awe of her power at yarning and less wary of her temper. Once he had happened on her napping in a garden chair, and had glimpsed the slack fleshiness of the face, the wisp of a hair on her chin, a rivulet of sleep drool trickling out of the corner of her mouth. Her vulnerabilities seemed to fit with her strengths, which left little margin for idealization, insisting instead on the truth, or as much of it as could be borne. But right now, he felt flattered. So she thought he was getting stronger! Did that mean he should argue with her more? He folded this exciting idea away, to unwrap and examine in detail when he was alone in the room he now regarded as his. Meanwhile, he was bent on winding their words back to his curiosity.

"So a yarn reflects not only the conditions of its yarner but the conditions of others the yarner has known?"

"Of course. Maybe in past—or future—generations. Or not known. A yarn imagines itself, you know, entangling out of separate strands." She held up her knitting, inspecting it. "Imagination can conceal while it reveals. Sooner or later, though, everything gets used." She put the wools down and stared at them.

"The yarns use up everything and everyone that any particular yarner knows or can imagine."

"Sooner or later, yes—if one has the fortitude to keep welcoming them. Unless of course the yarns abandon their host and flit to another yarner. That's been known to happen."

"I wonder, then …" He would start with the yarns and work his way in through them. Since they had never fully discussed the tale of the handmaiden of the holy man, he'd pivot from there.

"I wonder … Did you ever know a holy man?"

There. He'd asked it.

She didn't seem surprised. But he was, at her laughter.

"More than once. They're all over the place!"

"So … then … were *you* the—"

She coughed, peered into the basket of fruit, and chose a blood orange.

That route closed.

"I was under the impression," she said, stripping off the peel, "that you wanted to explore who *you* were, where you really fit in 'all this'. Isn't that what you said? Well, it's all there in the yarns. What's the point of exploring who I am? That's all there in the yarns, too. I'm just a yarner."

She could be a maddening, slippery fish—but he held his focus.

"So—if the yarns ultimately use everything and everyone, then are *we* bound for a yarn? Do you and I become part of the story?"

"Become?"

"Already are, then?"

"Fruit?"

He held out his hand, and she plopped a dripping chunk of garnet flesh in it. Sweet, edging on sour. Tart. He lay back down.

In a while, he was ready to try again.

"There's a recurring strand I notice in your yarns."

"Only one?"

"No, of course not only one," he chuckled, "many. But one seems to me a particularly strong thread."

She rummaged in the yarn basket at her feet and came up with a glowing skein of white mohair spun from a first-shear fleece.

"Something to do with ... trying to understand freedom?" she asked, holding up the pearl of wool.

"How did you know?"

She sighed. "Yes, it's a constant thread, my friend. I worry I might overuse it. Then again, it might be the sole subject for intelligent beings to consider. By the way, your curiosity about my life is really curiosity about yours. But that's understandable."

He heard her, but was barely listening.

She had called him "my friend." He felt a burst of silly delight. Then all at once he tasted that bitter pip of resentment again, lodged in the sweetness. Was he such a beggar as to be grateful for her friendship? Hadn't he earned it? Hadn't he earned the right to know at least as much about her as she knew about him? Come to think of it, she wasn't all that perceptive about him, either; she continually underestimated him. He should be more critical. She always said her yarns weren't perfect, anyway. And after all, he was growing stronger, she'd said.

"Your yarns are also quite … pastoral," he ventured, "Villages. Maybe the hint of a township or district. Interesting that none of your stories take place in the City."

She slid her wools down their needles, stuck the needlepoints into her ball of yarn, and let it rest in her lap.

The cat blinked awake into a coral yawn and an elongated stretch.

"The next story takes place in the City," she said slyly.

"Really? Why now?"

"Perhaps I wasn't ready to tell it earlier. Perhaps you weren't ready to hear it." She shook her head. "It doesn't matter, because from here on in, everything changes. By the way, we should go in. There's a chill coming on. Can't you feel it?"

"Everything … what changes?"

"Well, if you won't budge, then right out here—in what will soon be the cold and the dark." And to his surprise, she began:

"In a distant time, long—"

Now his anxiety boiled into irritation.

"It also seems your yarns are all set so far in the past," he interrupted, "Always 'in a distant time, long ago'."

She plopped her knitting in its basket. The cat took off, bolting through its favorite gap in the fence.

"Did I just say 'ago'?" She stood up. "Besides, what makes you think the *last* story took place in the past?"

"It was in the past *tense*!" He scrambled to his feet. Surely he'd earned his indignation.

"It was *told* in the past tense. That's merely perspective."

"But perspective is central to a yarn's structure."

"Depends on who's perceiving. Besides, perception changes whatever's being perceived, whether what's being perceived knows it or not. Or cares. All my yarns occur recently long ago right now soon and eventually! And why are you trying pick a quarrel?"

They stood glaring at one another.

He shook his head. He realized he'd have to rethink the whole last yarn—*all* the yarns, *again*—once alone in his room. Meanwhile, he would have to wait. Again. *Everything would now change, she'd said*. He would just have to wait.

"We need to go in," she said, "Darkness is already falling. And the wind is rising."

Silent, he followed her inside.

She settled down in the kitchen, so he did too. She took up her knitting and began to work, her fingers now flashing in a blur of movement and color. She asked him to build them a fire. He did. She asked him to bring out the wine, and to pour them each a cup. He did. Then he sat down by the fire.

He waited. He sensed an excitement crackling through the room, an anticipation of something about to happen. In the story? Beyond the story? He sensed that she felt it, too.

"This next story does not take place in 'ago'," she finally said, adding, after another pause, "and it takes its time, this story, so be patient with it. I probably should say that some might find it disturbing."

Some? But the tales she tells me are meant for *me*, he thought. And finally hearing a new yarn can't possibly disturb me. *Not* hearing a new yarn is what disturbs me.

But he waited.

"It takes place in the City. Also in the plains, coasts, mountains, deserts," she went on at last. "And it hasn't happened yet."

THE LAST SPEAKER

In a distant time, long years yet to come, the people had finally perfected an ideal society. Of this they were certain. It was a society forged to transcend identification with self, clan, or type, village or district, region or country—a society named, in self-description, Unity. The key had been forged during the centuries of stability—enforced stability but stability nonetheless—under the world hegemony of the Trust. From that came the aspirational process of merging toward the goal of one affiliation, government, currency, one social system, one language. Schoolchildren could chant the motto:

Unity is the answer, Unification the way,
Unifier the key to all we hear and say

More people congregated in cities now, though some worried that this came at the cost of a sense of place. It was undeniable that a uniquely metropolitan vibrancy bubbled through the stew: former hill people living as neighbors of previous valley dwellers, river folk encountering desert immigrants, coastal sensibilities blending with those from the mountainous inland.

As usual, this at first inspired fear, then enmity, then self-separation, groups clustering into discrete neighborhoods. But the government had counseled that over time all this would pass. And so it did, though never completely, a fact everyone tacitly agreed to ignore.

Hardest hit were the nomadic peoples, who were firmly—not forcibly but with an unspoken yet implicit threat of force—pressured to settle down, and who then found themselves privileged to receive special, relentless education in discarding their old ways. Discarding old ways had become commonplace, even fashionable. It was a trend bitter for most elders, savory for most youth. There were transitional challenges, to be sure, but the authorities were not insensitive to them.

One such problem was the diminishing presence, then gradual disappearance, of stories. Not that there was a public outcry about this vanishing. But a general, vague unease flickered through the population, an indeterminate hunger for something more filling than the sugary or spicy entertainments that proliferated in the absence of the old tales.

Those who brooded about such things—principled, thoughtful people, some of whom served in the government—felt a deeper disquietude. They feared losing the past, aware that without stories, history dims. They feared losing the future, knowing that without stories hope becomes an abstraction and planning an impossibility. More than either, they feared losing the present, living in the static of boredom, lacking possibility of movement or surprise.

The most eminent of these decent, concerned persons was a member of the High Unifying Council, a man well past 80 years alive, respected as much for his integrity as for his vigor—a powerful official still proud of his former facility with storytelling, however many years it had been since he'd made time to practice that craft. It was he who had driven the government to create the Ministry of Word Working, dedicated to devising sleek, modern stories in lieu of the old tales. Despite his age, he directed the ministry himself, exhorting his word workers to produce stories of brilliance and profundity that would enthrall, educate, and inspire the populace, as the old tales had.

This mission proved more difficult than anticipated. Story after story created by ministry workers failed to engage an audience. The new tales were as shallow and ephemeral as the popular entertainments, yet more pretentious: a compounded misfortune. When the word workers reversed direction, however, they churned out stories embarrassingly imitative of the old yarns though lacking their magnetism—which had after all accrued through millennia of repetition and variation. Nor did all word workers welcome criticism. The Minister couldn't help noticing that those who worked the worst superficial or derivative stories were most infatuated with their own words.

Yet the Minister—who termed himself a word worker, but was called by his colleagues *The* Word Worker, as if there were only one—had over his long life schooled himself in patience and flexibility. So he shifted the ministry's focus to scholarship, a discipline more compliant than creativity. Word workers were now tasked with seeking, collecting, and preserving the *old* stories.

This approach meant locating remnants of previously semi-isolated populations who held such stories among their lore. But that presented another problem.

Vestigial populations, though of necessity now conversant in the official language Unifier, had preserved their own stories in the myriad original tongues of their difference. And under mandate of the new society, those languages were dying.

It was regrettable, but die they must. Recent centuries of war had proven the need for only one communicative tongue. Differences in language had always expressed and reflected differences in perception, culture, even ways of thinking, which seemed to many people normal or at least innocuous. But whole industries of research now concurred that lack of communicative clarity stemmed not, as had been assumed, from how peoples interpreted the variations. Rather, the problem came from the variations themselves, exacerbating differences and, given time, leading to tragic hostilities with blood-saturated conclusions. This conclusion left the people blameless, so was contested by no one.

The authorities had expected to phase in Unifier slowly, but even the Minister was surprised at how swiftly the concept was being adopted and indigenous tongues abandoned. He knew that a language dies in stages, like a life form. First, it withdraws from public use to the sheltering hospitality of those still fluent in it. In the new regime of Unity, such people called themselves Guardians. Yet the most vigilant guarding cannot save an endangered tongue from increasingly dwindling into the private and intimate. It grows fragile, then feeble. No new words invigorate it, nor can it be comprehended beyond speakers who are ageing and dying. The Minister never failed to be amazed at the pace with which a language could shift its status, sinking from vitality to endangerment (the stage when the number of young speakers declines), then to terminal decline (when only elderly speakers remain), and eventually to extinction (when the final known communicant, termed The Last Speaker, dies).

Learning that a healthy language with thousands of speakers can collapse entirely in just two generations was reassuring to The Word Worker in his role as a member of the High Unifying Council. But it imposed a sense of urgency on him in his word-working capacity, and he recommitted himself to story retrieval in the shrinking time left. He dispatched his word workers across all the territories in search of Guardians and—should any be found—Last Speakers.

Their mission was complex, requiring delicate diplomacy. They were to save the stories of these vestigial peoples, but not the languages of the stories' origins, preservation of which carried a security risk of their revival, accompanied by who could foresee what violence? The stories were to be collected in the Unifier tongue, since no word worker spoke any of the moribund languages. Guardians, who spoke both their own vanishing languages and Unifier, could relate their stories in the latter.

The Guardians were cooperative, even eager, to share their tales, glad of the chance to preserve evidence of their culture from eradication. Most Guardians were old enough to have endured the wars and remembered the carnage. Some, aware that identity is one with its expression, had been drawn to join the underground in defiance. But language resurrection is extremely difficult and that adventure ended violently, with most of its members in exile, chains, or graves.

Both Guardians and authorities knew that as a language expires, much of the knowledge, history, art, and philosophy breathing through its stories and myths perishes too, together with the consciousness informing its unique structure, vocabulary, and grammar. So Guardians had come round, aware that their choice lay between sharing and thus immortalizing their tales, or watching this cherished lore fade into eternal silence. Since compliance had become the norm, it was rare for word workers to encounter a Guardian still resentful at being asked to surrender stories.

Then one day a word worker reported back to the ministry that she had encountered an uncooperative, even intractable, resister. It was not a Guardian, though. It was an actual Last Speaker.

This Last Speaker, living in a state of imposed settlement, was a member of a clan that had been part of a great nomadic people, one of the fluid nations that had wandered the territories since before recorded memory. Some formed caravans vivid with jugglers, acrobats, musicians, poets, and peddlers—all traveling, loving, and brawling together, hawking skills and wares. Most were herders, roaming with their flocks in search of pastureland uninhabited by, as they called settled peoples, Sedentaries. The process of Unification had fallen heavily on these people, whose experience had endowed them with such a wide view of the world that being compelled to root in one place carried with it an anguish keen as a lifelong prison sentence. Even so, no Last Speaker had ever been known to turn away a word worker on a story-rescue mission: Last Speakers were agonizingly aware of their predicament.

So this refusal was shocking. Nevertheless, the ministry sent a senior, more experienced word worker to coax forth The Last Speaker's treasures. When that effort failed, his superior was dispatched. Each returned defeated, reporting that The Last Speaker was polite but firm, making clear in fluent Unifier that the stories were not for sharing unless in their native tongue. Finally, The Word Worker sent his Deputy Minister who, though now old and ill, had been his closest friend since their long-ago boyhoods—substitute family, since neither had bonded with a woman or a man and neither had children, both having been dedicated wholly to their work.

The anniversary of Unity's establishment as a regime was approaching, an occasion at which the ministry planned to announce successful completion of the Great Culture Harvest, celebrating a catalogue of every tale ever related in all the prattle of languages, which would now be available in perfect Unifier, accessible to everyone.

But the announcement could not be made. There was the problem of The Last Speaker.

It did occur to The Word Worker's more pragmatic persona as Minister that if his Deputy could not succeed, unthinkable as that was, the public need not necessarily be informed of this holdout. After all, it wasn't as though anyone outside the ministry knew that this particular, problematic Last Speaker existed. Still, even in his role as Minister, The Word Worker was an honest man, and he found such a solution distasteful—while deciding that it could always be resorted to if all else failed.

Then news came that the Deputy Minister, while trying to convince The Last Speaker to do his duty, had suffered a seizure and died. The Word Worker was plunged into distress at this loss, only to then realize that 'all else' in this case consisted of himself. He would have to visit The Last Speaker in person. Might that actually serve, an aide suggested, as a useful diversion from his mourning? The Word Worker only scowled. He certainly didn't want to go. But he felt it imperative to fill in for his lost friend, completing that friend's final mission as he would have wished. This decision created quite a stir, however, since The Word Worker hadn't done field work for decades. Nevertheless, he survived the bustle of counselors disagreeing about his trip, and set out.

But when he and two aides arrived at the relocation site to which their subject had been assigned, no one was there. The Minister paused, mulling this over, then led the way to a little yard out back of the building. There, in the middle of the City, stood a small, sturdy tent.

"Nomads!" he sighed affectionately. He had worked hard to sensitize himself to primitive peoples, which is how nomads had been categorized. Now he dismissed his aides back to the street to wait for him there, and tapped the small gong at the entrance to the tent.

Before the ripples of sound had receded, the tent flaps parted. There stood a slender, short man, alive thirty years at most, with a smooth face, long hair that gleamed like black water at moonset, and heavy lidded eyes.

"You are well come," the young man said softly, speaking Unifier with the mildest flavor of an accent, "I was not certain you would." He gestured for his visitor to enter. The Word Worker stepped inside, taking in with a glance the minimal surroundings. A few cushions, a weaving. No visible cooking utensils, no chests, tables, chairs, bed. Nothing that could not be carried, perhaps in the few sacks that slumped, empty, in a corner. A double-edged blade of polished brass, like an oversize dagger, hung by a silk cord from the center tent pole. No one else was there.

"I am—" the Minister began.

"I know who you are, powerful sir," said the young man in his quiet voice, "You are the Minister of Word Working. You are a Senior Member of the High Council. But you also are known as The Word Worker. Some say you were even once a Yarner."

The Word Worker smiled. "You flatter an old man. I haven't been worthy of being called a Yarner in—well, never mind. Also, you have an advantage, since I don't know who you are. I am seeking The Last Speaker. Do you know where I can find—?"

"I am here, powerful sir." The young man bowed his head.

"But you are young! The Last Speaker is always old—sometimes older than I am!"

"I have seen perish everything that told me who I am, powerful sir. I am sufficiently old."

The Word Worker appraised the younger man. Courteous and restrained, yet there was something ... a suffering emanated from the nomad, like the trace of a dark, heavy perfume—even more intense than expectable in someone burdened with being the last of his kind.

"Forgive me," the Word Worker said. "And please—address me by my personal name. I am called Tayyaq."

"Tayyaq," the younger man repeated, "Tayyaq, Once Yarner. Please be in comfort." He gestured toward a cushion, smiling. The smile was subtle, promising sweetness. It made The Word Worker think of slow-pouring lavender-flower honey. Meanwhile, he knelt, gingerly putting down one knee and then the other, and with an awkward plop landing the final distance. He was now nearer to the knife, and he tried not to stare at it.

"It is a ceremonial object, sir. Your officers allow me to keep it, as they know I am a harmless man from a peaceable folk."

Reassured yet alert, the Minister said, "Well, I am not here to meddle with your cutlery. I am here to convince you to share your stories. And—may I inquire—your name?" he asked.

"You know it," the young man said, folding his legs under him and sinking in one graceful movement to a cushion. "The Last Speaker is my name now. In me alone live the words, stories, culture of my people."

"I meant your own—your personal name."

"I am sorry," his host replied, "You would not be able to pronounce it."

Careful to preserve his good-natured tone, the Word Worker protested.

"I have become something of a linguist during my years of harvesting stories for Unification. Let me try."

The young man shook his head somberly.

"I will not endanger you. It is most difficult for nonspeakers to pronounce. There is peril for someone who has not learned my language."

"My Deputy was a great semantics scholar. He—"

"Your Deputy Minister was insistent to pronounce my name. He would not heed my warning. Finally, I surrendered my name. He tried to speak it. He struggled and kept struggling. He wanted to … conquer my name. I could not stop him. His face grew red, then white. He strangled on my name, to my distress. Sitting where you are now."

The Word Worker sat up straighter.

"The Deputy Minister was my closest friend since we were boys. I grieve his loss. But I did not know such details of how he died … from merely saying your name."

"From merely trying to say my name. I would not expose you to the same jeopardy." The younger man paused, then added gently, "Tayyaq, Once Yarner, I am sorry for your loss of this friend."

The Minister cleared his throat. "How then shall I refer to …"

"I see. You wish to call me something. Name me what you wish."

Startled by such pliancy, the Word Worker stammered, "Well, I really don't … 'Brother', perhaps?" Both his Minister self and Word Worker self were pleased at the skill of this suggestion.

The Last Speaker blinked those heavy-lidded eyes. Slowly.

"Perhaps better simply to call me 'You'. Because 'Brother' is not accurate. 'You' is more true. For my people, to misuse words is to welcome harm into one's tent."

Tayyaq, stung again, nevertheless marveled how these smarts of rejection were soothed by a sweetness in the man's manner that shifted perspective to more important things. "You" would be difficult. But very well, he would try.

"How is it that The Last Speaker—that You—are so young? What became of your Elders?"

"They are unalive." The Last Speaker neither raised nor lowered his voice.

"And where have the rest of your people been assigned homeplaces? How are you alone here?"

"Also those in the fruiting of life. And the young, in the budding. All unalive."

"*All?* But that's—that's—How did they all come to be dead?"

"Unalive. It is a story. I can tell it in my language, but it would not be grasped by your hearing. Unless," he whispered, "Do you wish to learn my language, Once Yarner?"

The Word Worker leaned forward sympathetically.

"I can imagine how lonely it must feel, being unable to speak your own language to someone, or listen to it. No one, no one alive to comprehend …?"

"You misunderstand. I invite you to learn for your sake, not mine. I do speak my language, and I listen to it. All the day. When walking the City. When preparing food. When waiting for sleep."

"Ah. You speak to your ancestors, the spirits of your people."

"What would be that use?" The Last Speaker knitted his brow in puzzlement. "They are unalive. Why would a person alive be speaking to those unalive?"

"I thought … some cultures, some—"

"—primitives do so?" The Last Speaker's smile left The Word Worker feeling politely pitied. "No. I speak to myself.

I listen. I answer myself."

"What do you—What does You—say?" It was dizzying to address someone simultaneously in the first and third persons. Besides, he was still preoccupied with the horrible news that this man was not only a Last Speaker, but the last of his kind alive. The Word Worker decided he must task a deputy with finding some answers. What had happened to this entire people? Was it an infectious disease? Had they perhaps joined the underground and been wiped out? Hopefully, they had not been the victims of overzealous Unity forces during resettlement. Meanwhile, The Last Speaker went on, unperturbed.

"I say stories, naturally. Stories are the cloth from which our language is formed, as fibers are the fabric of your cloak. Stories are our lives, our selves, our way of being. Your people greet each other with certain words—hello, good afternoon-- and part with certain words: farewell, goodbye. We greet one another with the phrase, 'Shall we share stories?' We part saying, 'Until we share stories again'. All my people are in our stories, a multitude of tales. Stories are light to carry, and this is our great wealth. We are—were—called The People of Stories."

"And all of your people had the gift for storytelling?"

"No. Some were never able to unearth their stories, to discover themselves. That saddened them gravely. But they labored to replace that loss, acquiring great craft in retelling others' stories, and in deliberately inventing their own and themselves. We respected them. Then there were a few— three or four in all my living—who suffered both losses. They could not find their stories but also lacked the discipline to acquire the skill of invention. They were unhappy as part of our people. They had to leave us."

"You sent them away?"

"It was their choice. They became Sedentaries. We wished them no ill. But," he waved his hand, as if flicking away a moth, "they had no stories. They ceased to speak our tongue. They became unalive."

The indifference was smooth and cool as marble. The Word Worker took a deep breath, then resumed his mission.

"You. You are clearly a person of intelligence and dignity. Yet You refuse—refuses—to save those stories in Unifier. If stories are your language, are as you say virtually inseparable from it, isn't it all the more crucial to preserve them? I cannot understand how such a wise person can let his people's record of existence vanish. Do you not care for your people?"

He instantly regretted his question. But The Last Speaker grew even more still, as if he himself were marble, as if he were drawing those accusatory words into himself, as if he were a magnet for filings of pain. Finally, he replied.

"Hear me, Once Yarner. You swim in the current of your people, as I do of mine. We are each an instrument of our peoples. They choose, and we act so that their choice becomes real. This may be a source of greatest joy at times, at others a source of greatest despair. But always it is our duty—our story, yours and mine. Strengthening your Unifier, that is the task placed in your charge. Protecting our stories from defilement—stories of value greater than the glowing stones treasured in your City galleries, because these stories contain our lives—that is the task that was placed in my charge."

The Last Speaker closed his eyes. Suddenly he looked old and weary. Then, just as his guest was about to speak, he opened his eyes and went on.

"Still, once not-told, stories are all the same. Even ours. Only the telling, the How, makes the difference. For our stories, our language is necessary. It *is* the How. And though that language would take years to learn, such learning also is the How."

Flailing under the logic of such illogic, the Minister felt a need to take charge. "You. I would love to learn your language," he stated firmly, "But—"

"I am feeling that your words are a part misuse of truth," his host interposed in that same even tone. "I am feeling you intend me well. You value me, I believe that. But as a piece of art in one of your museums: valuable, breakable, truly appreciated only by someone like yourself. Please inform me, am I feeling inaccurately?"

The sophistication of this affably delivered rebuke so unsettled the Word Worker that he found himself retreating into his rank.

"It is impossible for me to abandon my work to learn your tongue, however great the rewards. Besides, you are—You are already fluent in my language, in Unifier. I beg you, *You*," he cajoled, "Let your stories live free from the tongue of their making."

"Can you live free from the air of your breathing?"

The Word Worker shifted uneasily on his cushion.

"Are you saying that all our work is—that all translation is at its core impossible?"

"No. It is possible to translate the content of a tale. But not the tale. And such halfwayness is not for my stories."

"Then they will perish. Will you sacrifice them to your pride?"

The younger man exhaled sharply. That shadow of grief again ...

"I have no foods to feed pride, powerful sir. Nor does it matter. Underground streams flow to the same sea as do sunlit rivers. Are they less real than if they had never been imagined? Someone will reimagine the stories."

"Reimagine them! Who? How?"

"Someone who will then be The First Speaker."

Tayyaq threw up his hands.

"You will regret this decision. When You face dying alone, many solitary years from now, with no one to speak to who can comprehend."

"I would not be alone if Once Yarner would learn to speak with me." A sweet, sly smile.

But the Minister clung to his purpose.

"My loyalty is to a larger goal," he frowned, "Saving the stories of all the lost tongues. It is my vocation. I do this for all people's sake. I am not free to go where I wish, do what strikes me as interesting."

"I understand well, Once Yarner."

"How could you, really? You are young. Please do not misinterpret me, but tragic as the loss of your people is, that also means you are free of responsibility for them, free of that pressure. "His host cocked his head, like a bird, listening. "You have no one to answer to. Besides, " the Minister continued, his tone softening, "my son, I'm in a hurry. I'm old. I already know six languages. I lack the time to learn yours."

"Why hurry if not to more fertile grounds? There are many different layers of time."

"Time is the same passage, always. Moments into years."

"Not to my people, powerful sir."

"Your people are—unalive." He stated it firmly, without cruelty. "Yet they could live again, forever, in your stories!"

"Why do you care so to save our stories?"

"Because I want the world to be able to share them. Because they are the particular genius of your language, which I respect. Because I respect all the lost languages, whatever You may think of me."

"I think of you that you made the law that lost them,

powerful sir. I wish to not be discourteous—but I am to trust your respect why?" The Word Worker bit his lip, but The Last Speaker went on in a contemplative tone. "As for example, Tayyaq, Unifier is not an enemy to me. A means for all to communicate, this is a fine story. One of peace, of health. But why erase the individual tongues? Why could they not thrive along with the common language, each enriching the others?"

His visitor's laugh was sharp and sullen.

"Because then most people would never use Unifier."

"No trust in those you claim to serve?"

"Those we serve don't trust us, either. People are … never mind. It has always been this way. We do the best we can, believing it's for the good of the people, even if sometimes it seems the opposite. We do the will of the people."

The Last Speaker contemplated his guest.

"I understand, Once Yarner, more than you might think. One can have power over others in the act of being enslaved to them. It is as if, speaking, one cannot trust one's own words not to mean their opposite. Still, it is sad for you Sedentaries. You are hardened, fixed. Not—not fluid, like water. Standing water grows foul. Also sad for *you*, Talaq! Carrying the weight of all those people's stories! Such a rich flow of difference to wring into one blandness. But since I am a primitive, I must ask: Tayyaq, why do *you* trust your words?"

This time the insult was undeniable—all the more since Tayyaq knew it was a genuine question.

"Because, among other reasons, I am not going to abandon the people of Unification. *Or* you, for that matter. But You, according to the records, vanished twice. We have had to bring You back to be resettled. Twice." Peeved at finding himself on the defensive, he had finally taken verbal aim and returned fire. Now he felt wretched.

His target offered a dainty shrug.

"I do not understand walls. I do not like them. You have me watched now. I know that."

"Never mind walls. We are here, in your tent, after all. Your place, not my place."

"This is not my place."

"Well, yes, that's true. As a nomad, you have no place."

His host laughed—a light susurration, leaves hushing a summer breeze.

"Tayyaq. You are a funny man! I have a place! You think we just wander about? It is comical, such learned men so uninformed! Our sense of place is merely larger than other people's. But our movements, though different for each clan, have patterns."

Tayyaq leaned forward. He wanted to get the nomad talking about his people.

"Our routes follow seasonal growth for the herds, whims of the weather, rhythms of the land. Each place is local home, in *now*, while we are there. But we do not own it, so there is no fighting over it. We revere no gods or ancestors. We honor only the local Essences of a river or forest. They are of a precise place, so cannot be adopted or stolen or imposed elsewhere. The journey is everything, you see, so everywhere is homeplace. Every alternate year we travel to a particular southern valley where we and other clans from our nation share stories while our herds graze the lush nettles. Another nation grazes herds there on alternating years. It took one hundred annuals of war and one hundred peace-meets to build the covenant tale for these pastures. Even fields have stories."

"So everything has meaning," Tayyaq said admiringly. "What a profound game to play ..."

The Last Speaker opened his eyes wide.

"Game?"

"Discovering the meaning of each—"

"*No.* Nothing has meaning. Only its story has meaning."

"I don't understand."

"Come with me, then. For even a short time. You have power, so we can travel wherever we wish. Let me show you the How of my language."

The Word Worker felt a surge of tenderness for this man, so naïve, this man who might have been the grown child he'd never had.

"There is no need to fear meaning, my son," he said gently. "Perhaps meaning comes from studying one thing or a few things, in one place or a few places, all one's life. Perhaps you think nothing has meaning because of all this flitting about in the life you knew. It's a matter of puzzling out the meaning— that is what constitutes profound play. Anyone who fears meaning doesn't know how to play!"

"It is not to do with fear, Tayyaq. And play is one How of our stories. But only one of many, while time is another. So is space."

"Space? Space has no shape. Space is emptiness."

"Space *between* is where all our shapes are born. Space between defines what forms form takes. Come. Let me show you."

Tayyaq felt an almost hypnotic warmth surround him, envelop him. He did want to know. Not for Unity's sake. For his own. Oh, he wanted so …

"Yes. Show me, You. Please," he heard himself implore in a high, piping voice, like a child himself, "But in a story. I cannot roam about with you. I can listen, though. I want—*I want to know You.*"

The Last Speaker looked long at him, his face a life mask of—was it tragedy or indifference, Tayyaq wondered. The black water of those eyes, deep enough to drown in.

"You cannot know me." He rose, in that fluid movement. "Yet it is a story that enters my feelings, a tale of Tayyaq—that you want to know me, that you want so much to understand. This story touches me. I can tell you only a story about the stories, not the tales themselves. That is reserved for those who can understand them in the tongue of their making. But I can show you a small How of our story. And that How ..." he cocked his head again, birdlike, "perhaps I might teach you a phrase or two that will not harm you to speak."

So it began.

Each day The Word Worker came to sit, aching joints forgotten, on the floor of a tent in the middle of the great City. And the City receded before the story that came alive in the voice of The Last Speaker. Sometimes the rhythm and lilt of that voice so overcame Tayyaq that he forgot to listen for meaning, lost in the music.

Through that music he roamed the massive stretches of the plains, climbed the snow-veiled mountain ranges and peered into hidden valleys, paddled down wide rivers to reach the great sea's mouth sighing its tidal *Ahhh* Shhhh, *Ahhhh* Shhh. He looked down as if from riding a wild hawk, seeing below dots of villages where people were working and laughing, arguing and sleeping, making love, killing, dying. He saw forests where the trees swayed as they inhaled and exhaled wind through green lungs.

"Nothing has meaning but in its story," The Last Speaker sang softly. "Words are born, like Essences, from the local homeplace, you see? There are thousands, more than thousands, of words for each thing—but always born from the unique homeplace. A river people will have many names for water, as will a coastal people, yet both have only a few words for sand. But a desert people has hundreds of names for sand, for the storms of sand and grains of sand, for its temperature and type and how sand shifts and the shapes it takes when it settles in drifts and dunes. A mountain people, especially in the far northern regions, will have a thousand names for snow. So it is with valley peoples, hill peoples. And with us, whom you call 'nomads'."

The Word Worker sat rapt, listening.

"Words also are nomads. They can move anywhere, like my people. If a caravan of nomads moving through desert peoples' regions rests with them awhile, when the caravan moves on it carries with it not only fine glass blown by the desert people from sand and fire, but also words for glass. Words go everywhere, but each is born from a specific homeplace. So today I will teach you a simple phrase. One you can pronounce in safety. *Tiasone aymay issah kae.*"

"*Tiasone anaymay isah.*"

"No. *Tiasone aymay issah kae.*"

"*Tiasone aymay issah kae.*"

"Good. Practice that."

"What does it mean?"

"Practice the phrase. Do not worry about the meaning yet."

The next day the story resumed.

"Some of our clans carry many dozens times dozens of members, others are small, though equally valued. Some have separate languages for female and male, others have no distinctions or even words for female or male. My clan had no use for the future tense, because we moved continually into the future, making it present. But the past tense, ah, such gradations! There was a moment or two ago; there was the recent past; there was a further past, a distant past, even a mythic past, when the story is so ancient it no longer needs new truth or description to freshen it because it has

that deeper truth whose power sustains itself despite—
or because of—so many lifetimes of repetition. And there is
the unknowable past, the past of all origins. The telling of a
story with no beginning. Or ending."

"But surely, every story has an ending?" The Word Worker
was loath to interrupt the music, but curiosity drove him.
"I still chafe at waiting for the end, as I did when I was little,
to learn what happens."

"But the ending happens throughout a story, Tayyaq.
Think. One gazes at a picture. The image can be perceived
in one moment, entirety and details, though the longer one
looks probably the more one sees. But a story exists in time,
through and across time. One cannot perceive it in a moment.
So why be impatient for some ending when all might seem
clear? Think, Tayyaq. A piece of music, a song. It too exists
in time, but does anyone imagine that the point of a song, its
meaning, is simply to arrive at its end? Music's tale unfolds
in each instant of playing, of listening. This also is the story
of aliving, Tayyaq. If too absorbed in a wait to make sense of
everything, one forgets to be alive. Each hour. Each tale. This
is the way a child of my clan learns—learned—to glimpse the
story and the How at the same moment. As if watching the
individual bird and also the flock swarming." He peered at his
guest. "But now is a moment for another phrase."

The Word Worker was startled by the change of course.

"Let the sounds into your inmost ear. They will draw you
in to enter the words. You remember the first phrase?"

"*Tiasone aymay issah kae.*"

"Good. Here is another. *Leton ayna ossah kwae.*"

"*Leton ayna ossah kwae. Leton ayna ossah kwae.* And what
does that mean?"

"Meaning, meaning! Practice the phrase."

"But how am I supposed to—"

"The meaning will open to you in time, as you enter the words."

"You want me to enter your story. You want to keep me in there."

"No, I want you to move about, and in your own story. It was you who forced me to fix in one spot."

"What if I want to get out of my story?"

"One can always find a way out. Choose another story, the story you think is you. Choose the story that brought Once Yarner to this moment."

"I haven't … It's been years since I spun any … I … very well." He realized he was nervous. He cleared his throat. "When I was younger I … chose a certain path. It was a path that led not to what was necessary, but to what was possible. To choose otherwise seemed at the time a self-indulgent imposition of what I personally valued over what everyone else valued. What, after all, was the use of inventing stories when real life could be invented, life without war, hunger, pain, disease, fear? What greater use for creativity than to transform it into power? I could not settle—for that was the way it felt—for creating stories and songs when a different *reality* needed to be created. At first—in fact for years—I told myself I could do both, one set of creations feeding the other."

"And so a Yarner came to be a Minister."

"No, that was later. It happened gradually. I barely noticed that I … it was wartime, a period so different from now, so terrible, that I can hardly count the …" He drifted off, staring into his memories.

"Come back to me, Once Yarner, return to now. Counting and measures also are different for wandering peoples. Like space and time."

The Word Worker rubbed his eyes.

"How can that be? We talk and talk, You and I. But sooner

or later we return to this same spot and same questions."

"Yes, we sit and we talk, as people have done and will do through what passes for history. But all the while, different histories are making themselves around us. Geological history, planetary history, astronomy, on into the unknown. Also, more small, more simply, this moment is right now happening with much different meaning for others. Somewhere, people gather for a ceremony. Somewhere, a woman rocks a restless child. Each in a space and time differently shared. Do you wish to know time as my people do, see why we understand it has no meaning?"

"Convince my painful joints of that," The Word Worker smiled. But The Last Speaker only replied, "They would ache indeed, were you to feel yourself walk through millennia. Let me show you by the telling of it. I have given you a How story about my people's home, our words. This now will be a How story about time. This one content of a tale I will try to sing you. But remember, the content is not the story."

So it continued, day after day, as the two men sat in the small tent, muscles at rest except for those needed to tell and those needed to listen. It was words that guided them to hike the deepest canyon known: a climb through the ages. Far below them, igneous bedrock—coal black schist marbled by fingers of rose granite—towered down the earth's core, forming the base for 200-foot-high cliffs of sandstone, which in turn swept upward a 650-foot thrust of shale, topped by 700 feet of vermilion limestone ridges layered in ruffles, crowned by 800 feet of yet another sandstone swirling into laminations of still a different shale—and another limestone cresting that, and another, and another: a vast splendor unfurling up the canyon walls. Here was a geological record etched by time's cartography on dimensional scales too immense and at a tempo too patient to be grasped by the brain. Here was a chronicle of primordial mountain ranges shuddering up along fault lines only to erode into plains later flooded by warm seas that would recede in drought to spread deserts in their wake to be flooded again, desertified again, flooded again—an innumerable company of motes dancing through rhythms of identity: lava cooling to scoria, mud hardening to shale, dunes crisping to sandstone, legacies of extinct sea creatures bequeathed to limestone tooth by shell by bone. Then—in the yesterday of a mere 10-million-years ago—the trickle of a river would begin to sculpt the emerging masterpiece.

The two men progressed as if moving slowly, step by cautious step, word by perilous word, the younger deliberately holding back so that the older, laboring, could keep up. They climbed through seasons as well as eons, shimmers of late summer heat that gilded the riverbed floor below crystallizing to cool, crisp air at higher reaches. They climbed through timespace, every thousand spans of elevation equaling a further journey northward.

"You glimpse the How we tell about time and space?"

The Word Worker sat speechless.

"You do see. Perhaps also you begin to see why there are only five or six stories in the world. The rest is in the telling." The Last Speaker studied his stunned guest. "Tayyaq," he said, "I have another phrase for you to practice: *Etya jheto ayna jehet.*"

The Word Worker gaped at him.

"Come, repeat it, please. *Etya jheto ayna jehet.*"

"*Etya jheto ayna jehet.*"

"Yes, good. Practice that, along with the first two. Then I will teach you a fourth phrase, a final phrase."

The Minister started as if from a trance.

"Why a final phrase? Why a—"

"Because my stories are now done."

"That cannot be. You are a true storyteller, even in a second language. In your mother tongue you must be spell-binding."

"Come with me then. Learn to hear that."

"To roam about, wildly? I cannot."

"Then let me go alone."

Ah, thought Tayyaq, *there it is*. "I may not," he said aloud.

"Who would it harm? I am one. You are many. Let me go free."

"You are free here."

The Last Speaker glanced around the small tent, then turned a face tightened in pain to his guest.

"I will escape. You know this."

"I know you will try, though you have every comfort. But you understand that you are watched. There are guards."

"There is no comfort for me here. And where I go no guards can find me."

"Come now, you are young, with your life before you. With such skill, You could be famous and well followed. Besides, any attempt to kill yourself would render this story of your refusal meaningless."

"Yes. It would."

"But You could give it meaning by sharing it with the world. By not being so—selfish."

"Selfish? Is that how you imagine me?"

"I *see* you, I don't imagine you!"

"Oh yes, you imagine me. Myself, I am only a story fragment in a vanished tongue." The heavy-lidded eyes blinked slowly. "Say to me the phrases, please."

"The phrases? Oh. *Tiasone aymay issah kae Leton ayna ossah kwae Etya jheto ayna jehet*." Annoyed, The Word Worker rattled them off, sing-song.

The Last Speaker frowned.

"Why do you rush through them, Minister?"

"Because I've learned the sounds by rote but still have no idea what they mean. Nor will anyone else know what I mean when I say them. Is this your revenge? Only you in the whole world understand what I am saying as I speak them. Otherwise, I'm alone with these words, horribly alone. It's like a punishment, a crushing weight to bear, a—"

He stopped, remembering that his host was a Last Speaker. Embarrassed, he struggled to his feet. The Last Speaker watched him in silence.

In silence, The Word Worker left the tent.

Whenever he returned from the tent to what he had previously called the real world, that world seemed drained of color, never more than this evening. Later, it occurred to him while in bed staring at the grey ceiling that he must ask The Last Speaker why this was the case.

The next morning, he recalled thinking this, and though aware of the irony in trusting he would receive an honest reply, resolved to ask after all. As he tapped the small gong at the entrance to the tent, he was in fact looking forward to an answer that—whether profound or nonsensical—he didn't doubt would be true. He was also looking forward to reconciling, since they had parted coldly the day before.

But no one came to admit him. He tapped the gong again. Nothing. Alarmed, he parted the tent flaps, entering to see the young man lying on a palette in a corner of the tent. He moved to The Last Speaker's side, saw that the man was covered with sweat, and touched his forehead—to feel almost singed, so high was the fever.

Behind the glittering eyes, urgency burned.

"The fourth phrase, the fourth phrase," he kept repeating. *Odyaira aymay neh tielet. Odyaira aymay neh tielet.* Say it after me."

"*Odyaira aymay neh tielet.*"

"Yes. Now say them all."

"Tiasone aymay issah kae. Leton ayna ossah kwae. Etya jheto ayna jehet. Odyaira aymay neh tielet."

"Yes, yes." The Last Speaker exhaled the words, barely audible, "You must practice them daily until they let you in. Do not forget them. They will …" then he fell back onto his palette and lost consciousness.

For the next however many days—Tayyaq lost count—he summoned the finest doctors bringing the most advanced remedies, to no avail. For the next however many days, Tayyaq never left The Last Speaker's side, bathing him with cool linens soaked in rosewater, whispering to him again and again how life was the most precious of stories, how he must live to tell his tales.

Yet The Last Speaker sank deeper into delirium. He lay in a half-coma, lips moving incessantly. The Word Worker leaned close, straining to hear. But these mumbled words were in the language he'd never learned, and the gates that had opened the path to that knowledge were now closing. In the tent's dim light, The Word Worker sat practicing the phrases he had been given, repeating his litany like prayers to a god who speaks a language unlearnable by its petitioners. There was nothing he could do to stop the inevitable. The Last Speaker was escaping him.

Then, suddenly, the younger man opened his eyes. He fixed them on the Minister.

"Once Yarner," he rasped, "Once Yarner. I speak to you in Unifier."

Tayyaq leaned nearer.

"Yes," he said eagerly, "I'm here, my son, I never left, I'm here."

The Last Speaker tried to form words through his dry, cracked lips. "The phrases?" he whispered.

"*Tiasone aymay issah kae. Leton ayna ossah kwae. Etya jheto ayna jehet. Odyaira aymay neh tielet.*" They came out smoothly this time, like a lullaby.

The Last Speaker sighed, "Well spoken. *Odyaira aymay neh tielet.* Yes." He struggled to sit up. Waving off the useless, hovering doctors, Tayyaq braced himself so that the sick man could lean against him. He held him in his arms as the younger murmured through labored breathing—to him?—it must be to him, it was in Unifier.

"*This was my story.*" A spasm shook his body. "*I was designated The Last Speaker. I drew the lot.*"

Tayyaq bent close and gazed into those dark eyes as if wordlessness could reveal whatever secret words could not. But as he watched, the light of sentience drained from the pupils that now stared, flat, at him. The body slumped in his arms.

He closed the eyelids. Then he sat for hours, cradling his burden. His burden? His friend. His almost son. This wise, supremely gentle man he had thought naïve. This primitive so civilized he would not survive without his own voice. This wanderer whose last words were in an alien tongue. The Word Worker wept.

But he was an old man, experienced in loss. He knew what must happen. So finally he roused himself. He gave instructions for disposal of the body. He lifted down the brass dagger hanging from the silk cord, to cherish as a keepsake. And he left the tent for the last time.

But mourning tracked him. Mourning deepened as the days and weeks passed—though whether he mourned more for the man or the stories that died with him, Tayyaq couldn't tell. Obsessively now, he practiced his phrases, terrified he'd forget them before learning—how he had no idea—what they meant. Still, they were all that remained of a man he now knew he had loved.

He summoned former Guardians of all known now-illegal languages to see if his phrases were recognizable in any dialects, but none were. Yet how could he be certain of this? The Guardians, no matter how assured of their safety, were too fearful to speak anything but Unifier in his presence— so he was trapped in the powerlessness of his own power. He tried to break his fixation by immersing himself in work. But there, facing him, were painful reminders: translated, uniform contents of what had once been a multitudinous variation of old tales. The content was not the story.

He resigned from the Ministry. He resigned from the High Council. He devoted himself to research, poring over volumes of dead languages. He could find his phrases nowhere.

So he left the City. He journeyed to the previously nomadic regions through which waves of the great wandering clan nations had once swept. Now they were settled peoples. But even in the towns, something glimmered, quicksilver, in their eyes, a wildness carefully lidded.

In each place he stopped, he left a small tribute—a bird's feather, a flower petal—in memory of The Last Speaker and to honor the Essences of the area. In each place he inquired about the particular clan to which The Last Speaker had belonged. No one could tell him anything, nor could he discover why.

Then, one night, trying to recall the dream that had wakened him, he instead remembered something else. He sat upright in bed.

There were living members of that clan! The Last Speaker and his people regarded them as unalive, but there *were* those few who had neither found their stories nor been able to invent them, who had left to become Sedentaries.

He jumped out of bed, exultant. During the transition when The Trust was phasing in Unification, every person had to be registered, by law. It shouldn't be difficult to find an exile who had relinquished The Last Speaker's language but still *knew* it, who could tell him what the phrases meant!

Hurrying back to the City, he grinned to think how he still retained powerful connections. Indeed he did, so it took merely a day and a half before a slovenly, middle-aged woman was brought to see him.

She shuffled along, hunching slightly—whether from lameness or servility he couldn't tell. Her skin was sallow, she sniveled and wiped her nose on her sleeve. Her coarseness was the opposite of The Last Speaker's effortless elegance.

The Word Worker leafed through her documents. Surprisingly, since she looked much older, she had only 34 summers. Poor. Seven children. Abandoned by the mate, a male. Charged four times with public drunkenness. One of those who had fallen through a gap in Unity's social programs. One of those The Last Speaker had described as being dismissed from the clan because of inability to find a story or a self. The Word Worker ordered food brought and watched her gulp it down, shooting frightened glances at him as she ate.

"Slowly, no need to rush," he counseled, wrestling to contain his own impatience. "I will help you. I will send you home with more food. With wealth, even. Here!" He dangled a purse of coins. Grunting, she grabbed at it. She seemed almost feral.

"Not yet," he snapped, yanking away the purse. "*You* help *me* first. I want you to translate something from the language of The People of Stories."

The woman flinched as if struck. Then she scowled and shook her head fiercely.

"Yes," he said firmly, "They were once your people."

"*Please?*" She cringed, whimpering in Unifier. "I cannot remember. I cannot speak it."

"I know you can. Surely you remember enough of it. I need only four sentences."

"I *cannot*," she whined. "It is not *permitted*."

"I say it is."

Silent, she stared down at her hands, curled as fists in her lap.

"Do you know where your people are?"

She twisted the dirty, tarnished chain around her neck. He reached out and grasped it, to examine a letter dangling there. It was a U. For Unifier? Surely not. Unity had never issued such identification. Then he got it. Unalive.

"Your people are unalive."

She nodded.

"Not like you, cast out. Truly unalive. Forever. All of them."

She nodded, unsurprised, her glance flickering around the room, seeking a way out.

"You know that? How? How do you know they are all unalive?"

She mumbled.

"What did you say?"

"A person … hears things."

"Ah." He was curious, but the original curiosity overrode the new one. "So then you know there is no one left from The People of Stories to blame you for helping me. They are all gone. But I am here—and I am generous. There will be more," he jangled the purse, "of this. Your children would never lack food again. You would never lack wine."

A quick glare at him before she jerked her head down again. Something gleamed in those eyes that recalled another gaze, black water at moonset, deep enough to drown in, carefully lidded. He flushed with a shame he hadn't felt since … but he couldn't stop. Not being able to stop turned the shame to anger. Suddenly, he was yelling.

"*Tiasone! Aymay! Issah! Kae!*" He hurled each word at her like a stone. "*Leton ayna ossah kwae! Etya jheto ayna jehet! Odyaira aymay neh tielet!*"

She gasped. He hunched forward, trying to follow the twitch of expressions playing rapidly across her features. Shock. Fear. Astonishment. Something—connecting … was it recognition? Cunning? Then—a blank. Lidded. Closed.

"*Tiasone aymay issah kae. Leton ayna ossah kwae. Etya jheto ayna jehet. Odyaira aymay neh tielet,*" he repeated, relentlessly.

She scrutinized the air into which he had released the phrases.

In a hurry now, he jingled the purse in her face.

Without warning, she shoved back her chair and lunged to stand face to face with him.

"I know what you offer!" she shouted, "I am human! I am not a beast!"

He was taken aback, but he rallied.

"Then why do you hesitate?"

She slumped again, retreating to the chair.

"I … it has been so long a time …" She bit her lip.

"If you do this, I will help you and your children, protect you."

She sat, head in hands, fingers covering her eyes as if trying to not see something.

"Children need protection, don't they?" he went on, "They can fall ill, they can … one never knows. Harm can come so easily … to children." Stunned, he heard the threat in his words. Disgust rose in his throat, he felt dizzy and nauseated.

But revulsion couldn't compete with the famishment: to *know*.

She stared at him. Finally she spoke, barely above a whisper, in a voice hoarse with fear and hatred.

"I cannot … get all the words. It has been years. I've forgotten … so much. But I can … I think I can give you the, the—"

"The *meaning*? The general meaning will do! Yes, yes, give me that!"

Another long look, blinking slowly, once, twice. She drew a deep breath.

"It is a verse. It is—ahh—the phrases are … directions."

Eager, he leaned forward.

"What? Like a map? Tell me!"

Haltingly, she began.

"When—no—*Where* … where there is a tall hill, ummm … this hill wears ice and snow … *Tiasone aymay issah kae*—it is a journey, you must go there. Then, something about shadows—the hill is so tall it casts a near valley in shadow year-long. You must find this place, it says, find this valley where no sunlight falls—*Leton ayna ossah kwae*. In this valley … a crop is ripening, one like no other crop. *Etya jheto ayna jehet. Etya jheto ayna jehet,*" she repeated. She paused, her eyes shining. A furtive smile, barely a tremor, grazed the corners of her mouth. "I have found—"

"What? Tell me! What is it?" he demanded.

Her expression masked itself.

"—words, found my words," she said, "the words … taste … sweet in my mouth …"

"Yes yes, go *on*!" he cried.

"In this place, you must, mmm, gather—harvest?—this crop. It will feed you a clue … *Odyaira aymay neh tielet*—this will feed you the *answer*," she corrected herself, finishing triumphantly, "feed you what you need to know." She exhaled. "There. That is all. That is the whole of it."

A long silence followed while he turned the words over in his mind and she watched him turning them.

"Tall hill. Ice and snow. Must be the Northern Mountains," he muttered, "Has to be. Then a valley … find a shadowed valley … with a ripening crop despite the shade …"

The Word Worker exploded into a blur of movement. He rushed to the door and shouted for his aides. They came at a run, and he ordered them to assemble a traveling party for departure to the North early the next morning. Then he gave himself over to obsessive pacing back and forth.

"Harvest this strange crop … it will feed me the answer. The answer. It will feed me what I need to know."

He stopped in his tracks.

"It's a message! A message to me from The Last Speaker!" He began pacing again. Meanwhile, the secretaries bustled in and out, packing and being generally officious.

In the furor, he suddenly noticed that the woman had slipped away. The last he remembered of her was the look on her face as she watched him absorb the translation. She'd looked … satisfied. Happy, almost. It was tasting the sweetness of her language, she'd said—but he suspected it was more likely anticipation of payment. Then he saw the purse, still lying on the table. She must have been so frightened by the commotion that she fled without taking it. He would send it on to her, he thought. But after the journey.

The journey was now everything.

Early the next morning, he and his attendants departed. He pushed the traveling party hard, despite his companions' complaints. His own old bones were so weary that only fanatic curiosity still knitted them together. But when he and his group arrived at the Northern Mountains, it was merely to face the next question. Where to go from there?

They interviewed villagers in the foothills, some of whom acknowledged having known The People of Stories when they'd passed through in the old days. But they all claimed ignorance of any shadowed valley—until a young man announced himself as not superstitious and in need of coin lurched forward tipsily. He offered to lead them to a site that, according to him, everyone knew about but avoided. It was less than a day's walk distant.

The Word Worker would have left immediately, but his team all but mutinied. He couldn't sleep with excitement. At dawn, they set out.

When they reached the place, The Word Worker found it vaguely familiar, as if from a dream. Had The Last Speaker shown it to him during their story journey? Looking down from the heights, he saw a dreary plain at the bottom of a gully, so ringed with mountains that the sun touched it for less than an hour in summer and not at all in winter. Daylight down there was a yellowish grey. There were no buildings, not even a shepherd's hut, no ruins, no road. Nothing was to be found here, except wind combing the grasses of a wide expanse in perpetual twilight.

But The Last Speaker had mentioned unearthing a story. Whatever was here must be buried. And as the expedition descended, drawing nearer, The Word Worker saw the mounds.

Reaching the valley floor, he directed his men to dig. Some peoples practiced raised-earth agriculture; perhaps something had once been planted there, something he was meant to harvest. Or perhaps some treasure—not of gold, he didn't value riches—some treasure of wisdom, the answer to what he needed to know. He paced the site where the men were digging, reciting the phrases under his breath for luck.

There was a shout. Then quickly a second.

The bodies began to surface. One after another.

These were burial mounds.

Impossible, Tayyaq thought. Nomadic clans burned or buried their dead along the routes of their wandering, in— he felt the clammy air settle on his skin—in kurgans, burial mounds. But still, he thought, his mind racing to escape what his eyes were seeing, still, never so many in one place! There might be a solitary small mound by the side of a well-traveled route, but this ... this was a field of kurgans. The whole valley was a burial ground. This was not the nomadic way.

Yet here were the bodies. Some mounds had only one, others had three or four, some gave up a pair. More than two hundred, the men estimated, after exhuming the first threescore. Then they refused to continue the dig. The smell was too foul, the sights too hideous. Furthermore, they said, they had unearthed enough to perceive the pattern of horror.

All the corpses were in approximately the same stages of advanced decomposition—six to seven years—and had all died the same way. It took only a glance to see from their gutted chests that they had been murdered. Each had been killed by a violent stab directly into the heart.

The knowledge came slowly to The Word Worker.

It came in small pulses.

It came like poison working its way through the bloodstream to the heart.

It came like the first grey streaks of daylight reaching toward a condemned man being escorted to his nonexistence.

The unusual youth of The Last Speaker.

His final words: *This was my story. I was designated The Last Speaker. I drew the lot.*

The double-edged blade of polished brass hanging from the tent pole—the dagger The Word Worker had taken with him that now glinted on display in his private library.

The supremely gentle, wise, naïve young man so civilized he could not survive without his own voice …

That man had murdered these people.

Children. Women. Men. Entire families. Scores of them. The field was soaked with death. Patches of turned soil were dark red, not brown. The stench hung thick as the silence, putrifying the air. *There, that one*—with a blood and mud-stained ribbon in what was left of its hair. *This one*, still in swaddling clothes.

Here was the crop that had been ripening, the answer to what he'd been so sure he needed to know. The field was a massacre site, sown with ritual murder.

How had The Last Speaker buried them all? Or had they dug for him? As their numbers dwindled, had they still helped him, one by one, to cover the beloved flesh of their lovers and children and parents before he covered their own? *I drew the lot* to fulfill the extinction of a people gone mad, an entire people who chose to die rather than live unfree to utter themselves.

The Word Worker could not move.

I loved him, he thought. *Like a son. I loved a murderer, a mass killer.*

He screamed, startling the workmen. He fell to his knees in the reeking soil, he pounded his head with his fists. "Life," he whimpered, over and over, *"Life matters more than stories."*

But there was that soft voice, whispering in his mind: *Life is stories, Once Yarner. Only stories.*

He collapsed. They bore him back to the City. There they nursed his failing body. But they could not heal his mind.

I loved a mass killer, that mind chanted. *He knew I came to love him, but he lied to me. Or did he? I thought he grew to trust me. Yet the knife was there all along. But he didn't use it. Why didn't he murder me in the tent? Did he care for me?*

Inside that mind, inside that story, echoed the fourth phrase: *Odyaira aymay neh tielet,* the answer to feed you what you need to know. *The Last Speaker was addressing me,* he chanted in his mind. *Is it more evil to eradicate the existence of a people than to erase their means of speaking that existence? Are the two the same?*

They bound his hands to keep him from hitting his head. But they could not bind his thoughts. *What did he need to know? Who had he become? A fool, manipulated into thinking that a savage—yes this was savagery, these people were savages— was wise and profound? You could not trust them, after all.*

Wait.

Then how could he trust the woman's translation?

Hadn't she grown angry, shouting at him? Then she had smiled, almost. But surely that was in anticipation of her money. Yet she had not taken it! Devious, she must have cheated him somehow. Perhaps, after years of being unalive among strangers, she truly had forgotten the language. But then … could she have invented meanings for the phrases? Still, the directions she'd given him did lead to the burial grounds of her people. Or had she got that knowledge some other way, then grafted it onto the phrases? "One hears things," *she had mumbled. And that strange radiance in her eyes—*"The words taste sweet in the mouth," *she said.* "I have found—" *she said.*

What if she had finally found her story?

What if she had made the whole thing up?

He became convinced of her perfidy. Then he became envious that she had found her story, if she had; envious that she had found her self. But his mind ricocheted back to its search.

Had those four phrases been a gift to a friend, a gesture of trust, as he'd assumed all this time? Or were they a prisoner's curse on his jailor? Then again, wouldn't The Last Speaker have realized that The Word Worker eventually must remember there were still-living clan members, the unalive among the sedentary, bereft of stories, equally unable to speak their native tongue or to forget it?

Deep and deeper, the arguments etched grooves in his brain until they could think themselves despite his attempts to block them, get free, end it. *But the ending happens throughout the story*, he remembered. Now, having dug up bodies he dug up stories—from anything The Last Speaker had told him, from his own past—trying to make a line or image fit, trying to open what was buried in syllables and sounds. His nurses unbound him because he no longer pounded his head. He pounded those four phrases instead, muttering, "*Let me in. Let me in.*" He no longer responded to the honorific name Minister, or to The Word Worker, or even to his own name, Tayyaq. He called himself Once Yarner. He listened to the lines of the verse in the original, in his mind, night and day, his lips moving soundlessly with them.

Then, staring out the window one autumn twilight, he understood.

He was one of those unable to find his story or self.

He was in danger of being unalive. To keep from being unalive he must *invent* what he could not discover. And suddenly, how easy it was! As he wrote, he recognized the words as the message The Last Speaker meant for him.

Tiasone aymay issah kae
I was from the first who I would become,
Leton ayna ossah kwae
claiming to love those I struck dumb.

Etya jheto ayna jehet
It was I who plunged the blade through the breath,
Odyaira aymay neh tielet
to escape my own story as Bringer of Death.

That was the day he proclaimed himself by a new name.

"I am The First Speaker," he said proudly to his nurses.

They had no idea what the old man meant, or that those were the last words in Unifier anyone would ever hear him speak. After that he sat staring at nothing, his lips working silently. Visitors—friends, word workers, former students—shook their heads with sorrow to see him this way, reminding each other in hushed tones how brilliant he had once been, how eloquent.

One morning a few months later, the nurses, unable to wake him, reported that he had died peacefully in his sleep—though how they were certain of that none could have said. They found him clutching a piece of paper on which he had scrawled his verse, prefaced by the message:

Chisel these lines on my gravestone. This was my story.

The nurses turned the text over to the Ministry, naturally. Officials there decided it was tragically inappropriate—though not surprising considering the old man's state of mind before he died. Instead, they commissioned a marble monument shaped like an open book resting on a pedestal, to honor his lifetime of service to the Unity government. On the day and at the hour the monument was to be dedicated, the entire High Unifying Council assembled in tribute, before moving on to a lavish ceremonial luncheon.

Across the City in a bare room, a woman sat rocking a hungry child on her lap. The little one whimpered, peevish and restless, tugging at the plain silver chain around the woman's throat. But gradually he grew quiet, his somber stare fixed on her while he imitated her soft chant, trying to learn it:

Tiasone aymay issah kae
Leton ayna ossah kwae
Etya jheto ayna jehet
Odyaira aymay neh tielet

To live is to move, at rest or play,
at home in motion and free to say
'nothing to lose and little to keep,
tell me a story before I sleep.'

"*Odyaira aymay neh tielet*," the child repeated in his baby lisp, "*Odyaira aymay neh tielet*."

It was an old nursery rhyme. Simply that.

THE BEDROOM

There is harm here.

Emptiness. But no space. Flatness.

This time I'm done for.

Or is this the illusion of finality: even crueler.

No, cruelty implies intent.

This is who I became. Reduced to banal insights. Preaching axioms, embodying them: like the sole legacy of an old drunk laughing at nothing, or a despairing schoolmaster teaching by rote, a bigot numbering the beads of his hatreds, a player inventing the game's rules as he breaks them.

Everything empty again. Flat. Dark.

Wait.

Through the flatness, something bulges.

Dimension.

There is a woman. Her hair crackles with sunlight. She laughs. She laughs! A current buzzes between us, a sublime lust. Another energy, too, just flickering.

Tenderness.

We drift with it, sink into it. The current runs swift, rough, lazy, pools in eddies.

We sink through days and nights of hope, weeks and months of effort. Years.

"Hush," she counsels.

But I was born to sing. "This is who I am," I plead, "this is why you love me, isn't it? Isn't it?"

"Hush, my love," she says.

I hush.

There is no hush in me. Still, I try.

We kiss. I hush when we kiss.

There is blood on my lips. Hers? Mine? Neither of us can tell.

Now she recedes, shrinking faster and smaller as she moves away from me. What is time but distance divided by speed? She is the period in a sentence, then the dot on a horizon, then the speck in a firmament.

"Someone should note this," I cry silently, "multitudes should weep for it, not just one man, alone, grieving …"

Space starts flattening back. But something new distends the surface.

Is it—? … Not her.

Something far glimmers. A book. Open, carved from heavy, pink-veined marble. Quartz? What a lovely word! The volume rests on a marble pedestal rising from a marble floor. They look to be all one piece of marble: floor, pedestal, book. The room is immense—a dim, vast hall, vacant except for whomever looks out from my eyes.

But the book glows.

I move.

Sudden.

So swift I miss the act of moving. I stand before the pedestal.

Shapes are carved into the book. Letters? Hieroglyphs? I know I must decipher them.

I cannot make them out. No. Worse. I can almost make them out.

I try to lift the book, to peer at it more closely. The book separates from the pedestal, after all. I must be stronger than I know, because the cool marble weighs so lightly!

There is a humming. Barely discernable, then growing louder. A resonance like that after the striking of a great brass gong, or like the hum of a swift current. The sound of wings, thousands of tiny wings. It surrounds me, it becomes a roar. I look behind and to each side, seeing only emptiness. There is a smell. Milky, almost bitter. I look up. No ceiling visible, only walls, high and then higher, intricately hieroglyphed.

No.

The walls are cells. An infinity of cells.

In each cell a tiny life form moves. I can see it! It bows, it gestures, it turns away, preoccupied with its existence.

I am in the center of one cell of one strand of one helix.

Each particle of energy in and around me is alive, complete, perfect, dying.

Three miniscule shapes emerge from different, distant cells. Slowly, they glide toward me, expanding as they draw near. They are of indeterminate sex and age, but they seem human. Each wears a dark robe with long, loose, hanging sleeves that cover any glimpse of wrist or hand; large soft hoods, worn forward, cover their faces. All three tread rhythmically, a slow, swinging gait, with heads lowered. They stand behind the pedestal. They loom tall before me.

They gesture to me, each motioning by the left hand, in unison. To me, and to the book; to me, and to the book.

"Read." It rings as a command. But not from them. As if reverberating from the pedestal itself.

"*Read*," it repeats, more loudly. I stare as the pedestal softens, grows supple, rubbery, uncoils from the floor. It expands, distends, elongates. It becomes a tubular, writhing shape. It is alive, growing: a grub-like, green-white, blind, winged creature. A horror of indifferent menace.

"*Read!*" Still louder, it booms and echoes. Paralyzed, I watch the shape swivel its head, rotate its vacant eyes toward me, massive wings flat. Its antennae probe the air, listening. Living rivers ooze from its body, rapids tumbling out an infinite froth of creation. The creature is bedded on heaps, hills, heaving mountains of eggs—as larva squirm through them.

"READ!"

In terror, I loosen my grip on the book. It crashes to the floor, shattering into a thousand marble fragments, strewn around what suddenly is a pedestal again. Nothing rests on top. Insect, larva—all vanished. Roar stilled.

One of the three robed figures speaks.

"Ahhh," it breathes. "Now you must reassemble the book to decipher the meaning."

I cry out, "That is not possible! The fragments are too many! Even if I could piece it together I could not understand the message!"

The figures sway from side to side, listening to one another through the silence. Then they speak, this time in concert.

"Ahhh," they sigh, with compassionate indifference. "You must. Or you can never return to your body."

They begin to melt.

The vast vaulted cellular walls also begin to melt, steaming into prisms of water shot through with dark radiance.

"The book!" I cry out. The book!

But my mouth makes no sound. Only bubbles rise from it.

I am swimming. I undulate, one long limbless spine of

rainbow-sequined ribbon twitching after each flick of my head, rippling through pleats of water. There is no pain.

There is no pain.

Above, bubbles O O O O O O O appear as I exhale. Odd, since I breathe water and color now, not air ... yet they form shapes, letters that swarm around me.

```
h   l   e       s       a   y   n   e   w  e
p     yi l         s     a       t       a
g     k     e   f   n   s   e   a   n  r  s
  t       w               n
d     n   s               n   w   s   n   e       m
  h
```

They dance and drift in sheets, they school and flock, curve, dart, quiver. How amusing that my bulbous eyes still can make out words, hundreds of words, bouncing around me.

It must be the puzzle.

There is *yes*. And *no*. There is *anguish*, and *rage*. I can spot *need* ... *shame* ... *risk* ... *heart* ... *strain* ... *poetry* ... *gone* ... *wisdom* ... *again* ... *poison* ... *eternal* ... thousands of words. But there are limitations.

I can make *other* but not *you*, for example; *wish* but not *question*, *whole* but not *zero*.

Still, I can string together phrases: *noon wakened streets* ... *does no one know how* ... *the poised agony of a lark* ... *death weeps sweet snowflake rain* ... *not fearing why*. But these are only fragments. Try as I may, I can make no complete sentence that might be worthy of the marble book's message. For that, there seem always too many letters or too few. *Pain flows downstream along the sky* interests me, for instance, and is a full sentence—but it fails to use all the letters.

I try and try. Easy enough, since no time is here, and I can do nothing else, anyway. I am surprised that I miss being human. I vaguely want to return to my body. But am I not *in* my body—gilled, lithe, iridescent-scaled? Is the puzzle about that?

In time I can assemble all the letters, like a coral reef, into words that build a sentence, jagged but possibly habitable. The first ones are a spew of trite maxims: *We fools see only dark then, phases not sowing any moons new.*

But I am improving. And then I have it, I am certain! A bit oracular, but still … *When No hangs on Yes dream slowly of no points to waken as one.*

Forced. But not hopeless.

So much depends on the pauses you take, though: *When No hangs on Yes, dream slowly of No: points to waken as one.* Or *When No hangs on, Yes. Dream slowly of No. Points to waken as one.*

Still strained. But the best so far, yes?

No.

Nothing changes.

It almost made sense.

Not really. Meaning had to be imposed on it.

Failure. I concede my inability to forge any sense with the tools I am given. Yet if this is defeat it is as light to bear as marble. What does it matter? I am still alive, rainbow-scarred, one color changing among others in the prism-dappled waters. I don't care any more—not even about the message. If that makes me cold-blooded, cold-blooded fits who I am now.

Perhaps *that* was the message I was meant to decipher all along. Then again, such thinking—"I was meant to"?—is merely another sly way to inject meaning where none exists.

Who else has been making up the rules of this game all along?

I caught me. What's more, I don't care, it was frightening, but fun.

Wait. Something is happening.

The letters are assembling themselves into words. The words are assembling themselves into a sentence.

There. There it is.

Anyone who fears meaninglessness does not know how to play.

On the ocean floor, I can see—coral shards? shells? … the marble fragments! They drift toward one another, iron filings toward a magnet. They fit. They *lock*.

There it is, the book, reassembled, sinking in the seabed sand forever.

"Ahhh," someone breathes.

Is that me breathing?

I am four-limbed again. Human.

But oh, such hurt. Such heaviness, the weight of remembering. So many years of loss and being lost, running from something or someone, hiding.

And now I cannot return to being a cold-blooded innocent, unimpressed by awe. This is the evolution I sought.

The woman with sunlight crackling in her hair. Is she gone? Dead? Did she exist? She was that speck in the firmament, nonexistent before its signal could reach me. Now she dies backward through time as if, on some planet circling a remote star, an entire civilization had just winked out.

A ragged wound gashed in the earth's skin is the sole evidence a meteor burned out there.

Mourning spreads through me again. Familiar, grotesquely bearable. Salt in my tears, salt from the undersea depths where I darted free, breathing color.

Then dread breaks against the shore of consciousness.

I am heaving salt.

The knowledge crashes, inevitable, a marble weight on my lungs.

I am still heaving salt.

I am still serving my sentence in the salt mines as a political prisoner.

I imagined my freedom.

I imagined all of it. I imagined the woman laughing in sunlight. I imagined being nonhuman. I imagined sitting on a stoop with a yarner. I invented it all—stories, laughter, hearth, garden, quiet talks, silky wine, peace.

None of it was real.

Only salt is real. Only suffering.

I lunge up and out against the flat dark, salt crusting my lips, salt stinging my wet face.

The cruelest illusion is finality.

Then from the no space of no dimension, slowly.

Blur. A bed. A small room, walls and corners barely visible, lit by starlight ghosting through the little window. Focus.

There is a *Here*.

There is a *Here*, after all.

He dared not wake the Yarner at such an hour. He could wait, though, for her rising. He could wait in the kitchen, by the embers of the hearth. *Safe*, the bubbles had permitted spelling. *Home* they had allowed.

Slowly. Heart stammering, alien limbs shuddering. Slowly. Edge off the bed. Stand. Stagger. Step. Door. Hall.

A light glimmered from the kitchen.

She sat before a softly hissing fire. She was knitting at her new, quickened pace. The cat was stretched out, belly fur toasting toward the hearth.

Warmth flooded through him.

But the face she turned to his was unrecognizable: eyes empty, jaw slack, mouth agape, body still as if frozen.

146

Unmoving, she seemed to be probing the air, listening.

There are places in me, lakes of acid that spew toxic fumes, she had warned him, *There are people in me who kill and joy in it, or kill and grieve at it but kill nonetheless, which may be worse. I am the world in which those who inhabit my yarns live. Beware. It is a harrowing place.*

Then she blinked. And looked at him.

There was *Here* again.

"You're awake." He breathed it like a psalm.

"Seems I am." A sniff. A smile.

"Are you usually up in the middle of the night?"

"Not if I can help it."

"Then how did you—how do you *do* that … how do you *know?*"

"Mystical powers? Oh my. Hardly. Your screams. It would have been a danger to wake you during that journey. It was necessary to wait until you were done. Here. Tea? No, have some wine."

They sat at the kitchen table, sipping the wine, watching flame chase flame up the chimney.

After a long silence, she spoke.

"So that's what The Last Speaker provoked."

Then she added softly, "Don't you think it's time you told *me* a story?"

THE STRANGER'S STORY

When you look at me, you see a young man. Don't be deceived.

I am an old man, and I own nothing. Had I a legacy, that might be a story. But such a yarn is hiding. It belongs somewhere. Where do I belong?

So this story begins.

The stranger's story is the tale of everyone who cannot recognize themselves in it because they are confident they belong somewhere else.

This particular man had always known himself a stranger.

He had been born for it, raised not to fit in. Gift, curse, salvation, doom, it was his identity. His father was away or mad or dead: a memory brightly loving, also threatening, possibly imagined. He and his mother formed the brisk reality. They never had a home as such. They wandered, settled a while in one place; then, sometimes in the middle of the night, suddenly uprooted themselves—moving on as if fleeing someone or something. This life developed its own routine and rhythms that over time provoked in him pity (sometimes verging, it must be admitted, on contempt) for stayers.

Stayers settled, literally, for less than the world. Stayers settled not only for place, but for each other—huddling together in reassuring knots: kin, tribes, sects. Stayers often relied on fear of otherness as their clotting factor. But the pity he felt for them was laced with an outsider's envy, and he knew it. He solicited details about their lives. Though he bored easily, their stories interested him more than he had anticipated. So he came to perceive others keenly, though he was saddened by feeling himself unseen in turn.

He believed himself seen and loved by his mother. He also knew that she was stubborn, resourceful, given to strange dreams, and impatient—having, she said, used up all her patience when young.

So they journeyed through the world. His memories performed shadow-puppet dances of the two of them moving through towns and villages and cities, once traveling with a company of pilgrims, all of whose stories he collected, too; once living for months with a group of other women and children, to whom he learned he could tell the stories and feel as if he almost belonged. His mother might sometimes have gone hungry, but he never did. She worked as a fisher when they were near water, as a farmer during planting and harvest times, as a weaver, sometimes as a scribe, which she said her father had been. In one town, she set up shop as a baker of fig pastries—but her delicacies were so popular they became famous throughout neighboring towns, so she promptly closed shop and moved herself and small son along. Her array of skills that purchased their survival had astonished him when he was a child. In time he came to understand that this was simply her nature, and, finding himself open to his own expanding capacities, he adopted it as his own. Once, when they traveled with a caravan, a trader took a liking to this inquisitive child, gifting him with a wooden, five-stringed doola'h. Because it seemed easy to play but was not, it did not bore him. He taught himself to make music from it and to sing some of the stories he had learned, and he added that to his skills.

He never knew why they kept moving. She always said she would tell him when he reached manhood, and tell him other secrets—who his grandfather really was, who she was, who he was himself. She always made him feel they were special, which excited yet embarrassed him. Then, suddenly, she died, taking the secrets with her. Even her death, though unexpected, was impatient. She slipped and fell, hitting her head while scrambling down a hill to gather berries local villagers didn't bother harvesting, since the descent was too steep. She had set off at dawn, leaving him behind to help work the harvest. She returned at midday, covered with bramble scratches and complaining of a headache. She waved away offers of help, made a poultice for her head, brewed and drank willow tea, and pronounced herself healed. By night she was dead.

The villagers, regarding themselves as charitable people, stood ready to take in this suddenly orphaned lad, no longer a child but not yet a man. Still, he knew from past experiments at fitting in that his half-hearted attempts to belong would be received laughably at best, and as parodies at worst. So he buried her, and already aware that it can be dangerous to reject charity, he fled.

He mourned the loss of her. Just as deeply, he mourned the loss of secrets he now would never learn. He endured alternating fits of anger at her for dying before telling him what he needed to know, and guilt for feeling anger at her for dying before she told him. But in time he discovered that anger spent itself, if you let it, pulling guilt along in its wake. Even mourning was exhaustible.

He resigned himself to never knowing who he was, but he continued honoring his own uniqueness. As a child, he had lost playmates. Now he found himself losing companions, then colleagues, friends, lovers. But he gained stories; his collection grew. He would elaborate on them, merge them, play with their elasticity of ideas, telling and retelling and refining them to himself, alone at night, to keep himself company. Most of the time he chose not to betray being a stranger, despite numerous temptations to do so.

He avoided customs many still considered rites of definition for manliness: conquests of land, people, or both. They bored him. But he cared about others, cared greatly. He became engaged in the world, which was large enough for him to fit there, at least abstractly. He learned when to hide his intelligence, and how to make people laugh. He discovered how humor can be a balm for much of the suffering so common it passes for being awake. He found that stories and music made people recognize, at least for a while, their similarities, usually overlooked in the emphasis on difference. From all this, he reaped real pleasure. But gravity of human pain drew him in.

So he traveled the world, joining a shifting alliance of women and men trying to save it. He was willing to pay the price. During these years, he paid by being misunderstood, persecuted, beaten, and imprisoned. He was sentenced to hard labor in the salt quarries for some years. He lost everything but the doola'h, which he variously hid, pawned, bought back, re-hid, and finally rescued for everyday use again.

But to act in the world meant reacting, instantly. It always won out over the quietude needed while waiting for songs and stories to reveal themselves. The world's agony was always more urgent, more insistent, more compelling, and—yes—more rewarding, whether from witnessing the relief of those helped or the anger of those challenged, because that meant they had noticed. The world of action was also far more generous in bestowing a feeling of accomplishment, however slight or brief, than was his art, which remained forever unfinished, imperfect, in progress.

So he chose another path. It was a path that led not to what was possible, but to what was necessary. To choose otherwise seemed a suffocating imposition of what others valued over what he valued. What, after all, was the use of hopelessly battling the vagaries and cruelties of the social compact when entire dimensions could be invented, without hunger, pain, disease, fear? What greater use for power than to transform it into creativity? He could not settle—which was the way it felt—for creating flawed new societies that fractured into sour recriminations and corrupted dreams when a different reality needed to be created. Nevertheless, at first—in fact for years—he told himself he could do both, one set of creations feeding the other.

But as the years passed, although he felt no less commitment to the causes in which he had invested so much of himself, something changed. He felt a growing distance from such passions—though never from the melodies ghosting through his brain. He missed the feeling of accomplishment, yet now he held himself apart from causes, clinging to the knowledge of how fatal a harvest any well-being bought by others' pain could be. But he continued spurning charity—always earning his way and insisting on fairness for those wronged. Again and again, as if it were his personal adage, he said that charity humiliated, fairness dignified.

The truth was that he had not been able to hold to the path of being active in the world. Sometimes he felt this as a shameful failure, sometimes as a fortuitous escape. Other times, he felt he *had* held to it—but as another self in a different dimension, an echo of some song, a character in some story.

After periods in prison and at hard labor for his attitudes— subversive attitudes regarded as foreign agitation no matter where he went—he learned the desire for oblivion, which is distinct from Nothing.

When he discovered the virtue that can lie simply in daring to look straight into Nothing, he wondered if that meant he had acquired wisdom. But he was wise enough only to intuit that the virtue in daring to look straight into Nothing could, he suspected, lead to a swift exit. That might be acceptable, after all—maybe welcome. But not yet, he thought. The real virtue, he discovered, lies afterward, in not looking away.

So he traveled on, working at odd jobs, telling tales, restringing his doola'h and practicing, practicing, always working toward greater precision. This helped him not to look away. But it also took its toll.

He continued to collect stories about what he was learning.

He was learning that much of what gleams in the dark is decay, nonetheless beautiful for that. He once watched millions of tiny fish corpses bobbing on the surface of a tropical bay bead the waves with phosphorescence. He once saw a greenish glow hover above a marsh at night; the locals called it foxfire and told him it was caused by gases from fungi and decomposed tree trunks. He came to love learning how death illumines life.

As he grew to maturity, he found himself more and more disengaged from trying to heal the wounds of the world. This grieved him. But the wounds were always the same, the solutions were always evident, the energy expended on ignoring or denying the solutions always more demanding of time, effort, and resources than would have cost a fraction of the time, effort, and resources applied to actual solutions. He never ceased admiring those who persevered in the teeth of such repetition. In some different dimension perhaps his echo self was one of them, a character in some other story. He still believed such people carried the species forward beyond where they could see. He knew that many, perhaps most, were women carrying some even larger burden—which he understood he could not understand but had to try.

With women, with men, there were personal arcs of passion. There was thrill, anger, fear, and the silliness that intoxicates with pure glee.

There was one particular woman. She gazed at him with such an opacity of innocence that on the spot he loved her. She was not easily seen, nor did he look away. He learned love's tasks and tricks: how something deep enough can promise transformation—whispering *I'm really different this time, don't you see?* —but delivers so rarely one might miss it when it does.

He tried. He tried to become a stayer for her sake, to settle. He learned there are times when one mistakes ashes for embers, when the bearing of something and the understanding of it cannot be endured together but must take turns. He learned that not everything gets resolved, sometimes it just gets left behind. He forgot her every day for years after, since all his familiar routes and objects had become infected by her absence.

So he sought new routes.

His regrets were not for his past but for his future, which now looked bloated with the very solitude he had sought when crowded by her always almost changing. There were times when he fell into blaming, blamed otherness, strangers and settlers, blamed his childhood, his mother and the secrets she took to her grave, blamed the weight of the stories he carried.

But the challenge to work Something from Nothing obsessed him. It was why he could bear waking up each morning.

If no one tried to silence him now, it was only because they could no longer translate what he was saying into anything they cared to understand. Sometimes they even were solicitous.

"It is hard for you, where you are, yes?" they asked, wringing their hands, tilting their heads sideways.

"No," he replied, surprising himself. "What's hard is reporting back from where I am."

So, to himself, he told his stories and accompanied them with what had never left him, his sole constant, the music that breathed beyond politics or love. He had played many instruments through the years, but still had the five-stringed wooden doola'h. These days everyone thought the doola'h primitive, thus harmless, so no one tried to take it from him any more.

That is the dimension from which he gesticulates, as he staggers on.

Borders and demarcations blur. He knows they don't exist.

Except with regard to suffering. He knows indistinction is possible only when suffering is not acute. Once suffering has made itself known in all its clarity, being alive exists in black and white, exposing subtlety as a vulgarity of pastels.

Suffering rinses everything clear. It has one story. In suffering all acts exist with a single goal: to make the suffering stop.

These are some of the tales he has learned on the journey to where he is. He has learned that bitterness is easy; sweetness is what's hard—especially when false sweetness is so omnipresent it can sour anyone to bitterness. And he has learned to smile at that.

By now, everything he knows can be expressed simply: *Pain passes. What you do with it lasts.*

But he is drained by fatigue from rootlessness, and weary of his own stories. He has a pocketful of coins earned from playing the doola'h. He hears rumors of a place where stories rarely or never told any more can be heard. It's far off in the City, where he'd sworn never to go again ... but it's in the old part of the City, where the cobbled streets are narrow and quiet. He thinks he might rest for some days in such a place, might learn more, before moving on. He seeks out the place and finally locates it, at the end of an alleyway, in a small house with a little pear tree out front.

This will do, he thinks.

THE HOUSE

She completed a row of her knitting and without pause began another, from a skein that looked nearly used up.

"A little—abstract, your story, don't you think? Some lovely images, though."

"By abstract, you mean ... nothing really happens in it."

"Oh, a lot happens in it. More than you might yet give yourself credit for. No, I mean ... philosophical. But that's its own kind of story, too. Of course, it's a highly personal story, and self-exposure, while brave, often requires the sanctuary of philosophy. Then again, there's really only one character, isn't there? Well, three, if you count the mother and the woman—but they're both sort of shadowy, aren't they? Well, I suppose four characters, if you count the doola'h. But no ... *talking*, so to speak. Still, think what fun you'll have, working all that out!"

"What fun," he said glumly.

"Well, those who settle for virtuosity might be passing

up mastery. Oh, my dear. It's just not finished yet, that's all," she soothed.

"I thought you said no story ever really finishes. Or starts."

"So I did." She was knitting even more rapidly now.

"A really good story always starts in the middle, doesn't it?"

"How could it not?" she nodded.

"Did you mean it when you once said that I could stay as long as I liked?"

"Do I usually say what I don't mean?"

"No."

"Well?"

He had to smile. It wasn't as harrowing to be honest as everyone pretended.

"There's peace here," he mumbled, suddenly feeling shy. "I feel I've come home."

"So there is. So you have," she murmured. Her fingers flew at the knitting. "For now." Then she added softly, "By the way, I'm leaving in the morning."

"For how long?"

"For good, I think."

He stared at her.

"What?" He heard himself shouting, panic in his voice. "Where will you go? Why? How?" *Here* was crumbling.

"Yes. I don't know. Because it's time. Walk at first, then perhaps ride. Not sure." She had answered each of his questions in turn and he was no more informed than before.

He pressed down the panic. It was a puzzle, surely, maybe a new story. Or an old one, ongoing, merely told in a new tense. *All my yarns occur recently long ago right now soon and eventually*, she'd said.

He grabbed at a light rejoinder, trying to enter whatever story was getting itself told.

"So … will you explore what villages still exist these days? Are you going up the mountain path to build a hut at the top?"

She laughed, a bawdy guffaw he'd never heard from her before.

"Excellent! Yes, *yes*. Maybe waft myself to the future? Or join a caravan again!"

"Again?"

"You're not the only one who rode with a caravan, where you met your doola'h. That vase," she nodded toward the mantle, "comes from a caravan I rode with once, long ago. I bartered a story for it."

Here was back. He exhaled.

"A story you've told me?"

"No."

"Oh."

"Don't look so crestfallen. You know by now that the listener determines what yarns get told as much as the yarner does. In any event, I've no idea where I'll wind up. Truly."

"Are you serious?"

"Have you known me not to be serious?"

"But—you—you are—"

"Old? Yes. And in creaky health? Yes. And remaining safely comfortable at home is probably a better way to face ending things than someplace where one is a stranger?" He was really thinking, *where will I go? where can I be at peace now?*

"Yes," he muttered.

"You might know best, since you're accustomed to being a stranger. But I'm a stranger too, now, in a way—to age. It's an interesting new terrain. Humbling, for one thing, especially to anybody as intolerant of inadequacy as I am. You see, there's a raw young yarner, hungry for fresh patterns and colors, itching inside this soon-decomposing body in which I find myself on the way to your phosphorescence. She deserves attention, don't you think?"

It was as if they were meeting all over again.

"I've known you such a short time!"

"Well, a year and a day, come tomorrow, turns out. You arrived in autumn. But I agree. Ends always are such interruptions, aren't they? An end stops being an interruption only in retrospect, once one realizes that what *is* won't continue after all. What *will* continue, in fact, is the end. Amazing, how the one thing we can be sure of, the end, always takes us by surprise. And it's been happening there all along!" She bellowed that bawdy laugh again.

"Aren't you afraid?" He was single-minded, obsessed.

"Petrified!" she chuckled. "Do you think that should stop me?"

"Well, it might … slow you down somewhat."

"Then probably I would have been rushing too fast, I wager. I value fear. It's reliable—so long as one doesn't let it get possessive. Trust your fear, I say, and you'll be ready for most things."

"But not everything."

"Naturally. Then what would be the point of fear?" She chatted on, gaily. "For most of my life, I've done things I was certain I couldn't—did them anyway. Odd, now, to find some things I'm certain I can do, I can't. Age teaches you the most hilarious lessons about the practical limitations of power."

She made it sound like a story. He couldn't resist.

"For example?"

"For example. Lately, I've been rummaging through my drawers and closet, respectfully but objectively—as if I were riffling the drawers and closet of a dead woman I'd never met. Items, gadgets, *things* that survive, but only because they've never been alive. *So this is where she kept that, next to that, over here, under there, hmmm.* Looking through the eyes of someone trying to figure me out. Now *there's* arrogance for you, imagining anyone would care! But it's instructive. It teaches you the irrelevance of what you live with daily. Owning really is *such* a preposterous idea! When I was younger, the world seemed mine to own—and oh, how I wanted to leave my mark! Now I would be content to leave not a footprint. That much less work for waves to erase from the sand."

"Do you truly mean that?" he asked, wary of her snapping that she always meant what she said.

"Not sure," she surprised him again. "I'm wrestling with it, though. When I feel that foolish but powerful thirst for attention …" she flushed dark red. "I don't approve of myself." He had never seen her blush.

"It's just—human, I guess."

"You're being generous." She picked up her narrative, though whether to evade the subject or because of an imperative to move on he couldn't say. "I once had an urge to domesticate things, too. Now, except for the cat—who domesticated me—my pets are wild: the birds I feed, the strays who come and go. Perhaps I need to be wild again myself."

"But you are not *that* old."

"I'm earning age. No one earns youth, though too many older people today demand the chance to, so they miss what's happening now. Actually, one way to define youth is by its lack of capacity to envisage age for itself. But here's a secret: once you've glimpsed what it's like to feel old, it's difficult to fake feeling young again. Flesh is drawn to an inexorable gravity at the core."

"And isn't that all the more reason to remain here?"

"Perhaps. But frankly, my friend, I'm too tired to stay still. Oh, don't think I can't hear ahead! I can eavesdrop on my older, white-haired self grumbling backward at this grey-haired me, 'Well, that travel-into-the-world-be-wild-again idea of yours certainly demonstrated the idiocy of the young.' Then I might have to crawl to you as you once did to me. But—"

"—wherever I am, if you ever need—"

"—it's all relative, is my point. Aging. Dying. Distance divided by speed equaling time. And, for pity's sake, it's just *death*, after all," she added. Then seeing his stricken expression, "Likely a ways off. Green wood burns fastest, not seasoned oak. Meanwhile, why not? Mountains, caravans, deserts!" she laughed, "I might visit my children."

"You have children?" he gasped, "You never mentioned you have children!" It came out like an accusation.

"I never mentioned a lot of things," she shrugged, "They weren't the point. Yes, I have children. Grown, of course. A daughter and a son. I birthed the lad and adopted the girl."

"A son and a daughter?" He heard himself sounding angry, and realized with a sting of humiliation that he sounded jealous. He could barely believe she was opening facts of her life to him now, when she was about to leave.

"Who was the father—where—what does he do?"

"A decent man. Yet another holy man," she sighed, "long gone. My children live their own lives, a fair distance away. My son is an astronomer. Studies the stars. Uses such delicious words! Noctilucent—that's a nice one, eh? Means night-shining clouds. Even when he was a wee tot, you could barely keep him indoors at night, always peering up with those somber eyes into the blackness spangled with light."

"And your daughter? Adopted, you say?"

"Adopt, adapt, adept. Universes of difference separated by a vowel. My daughter adopted me. I never had the joy of her as a child. She was grown when we came to know one another, and she was recovering from a great sorrow. She had been at a place that housed and healed mendicants—the sick, the mad, and the needy—mostly women and children. There she had grown close, closer than blood sisters, with another woman. It was a storm of intensity. Then, one day with no warning, the woman was gone, leaving her a note that said such passion could not be borne. Strange, eh? Well, strangers aren't the only ones who are strange, and we're all strangers ultimately. But the woman who was to become my daughter was desolate. · She'd always been contemplative, but this transformed her into a yarner. Sometimes it happens that way, enrichment by loss. Her yarns are very different from mine. When she first came into my life, she stood under the pear tree and began singling out the branches, slowly, carefully, noticing and listing the unique details of each branch. I knew then there was a yarner in her. But it had taken desolation to bring it to birth."

"I envy you your family," he murmured, "I find myself longing for the secrets that died with my mother, longing for family, ancestors. Mostly for a beloved. And a child, perhaps. It seems I'm doomed not to enjoy that life if I crowd my spirit with stories."

"Hah. That's what women have been told all along."

"Maybe there's some overarching truth in it, then."

"More likely some overarching lie by a conspiracy of tellers who opt to cower out their lives in an either/or dimension of what's really a both/and universe."

They laughed.

"There's no mystery or destiny to it," she scoffed, "It's just extra work."

He was still fixated on her children.

"Do they have families of their own?"

"He does. She'd wanted children in her youth, she said. But apparently that changed after the death of a child she'd once grown close to in a village where she lived for a time."

"And … so … you will visit them?"

"Actually, I doubt it. It would be best to go with no fixed destination at this point."

"What point?"

"Precisely. I don't need a clear path now. Which is convenient since none are available. But you may need one, for a time. You've earned it. Odd … I assumed the inheritor would be female. Lack of imagination on my part!"

"What do you mean?"

"The inheritor. It's yours now: house, garden, everything. Until you pass it on, in turn."

"You can't mean that."

"Why do you keep telling me I don't mean what I say?"

"Well, at least once you didn't."

She sighed. "True, true. But you being the inheritor *fits*. It's time a man stepped up to the job, shouldered the burden."

"I can't possib—what burden?"

"You'll work it out. Finding your power, then volunteering it—that's one definition. Many people—mostly men these days, I'm afraid—assume others will pay the cost, risk the pain, forge the beauty, and in any case it's not their affair. It catches up to them, of course. Sooner or later, everyone bleeds sufficiently, whether they plan to or not. But as usual, women overdo it. So it's fitting you shoulder the burden. Power volunteered. Yes."

"But I have no power! What do I do?"

"Oh, small things. Practice the economy of kindness. If possible, find someone you can trust, and trust that the trust might not last—but don't let that maim your capacity to trust. Trust yourself. It's all up to you, to do with as you see fit. Look through your new house. Explore all the rooms! You'll be surprised, I think. Get to know your neighbors, too.

The old man three doors down has an interesting story. And just across the road," she prattled on, "lives the young woman who threw my blue pottery. She does fine woodcarving, too. If you offer to give her a story she might give you one of her flutes. They blow clear, true notes. She wears these scuffed old red boots, and the cat often visits her when—"

"But your children should have this house!"

"No, they lead other lives in other places. This house is not for them, and they know it." A half smile. "I knew the day you arrived it was for you. I saw the person I'd glimpsed through the years approaching that day. I saw my departure approach, too, in your arrival."

"Are you just … you cannot be just …" He couldn't say it.

"Getting out of your way? Some would think so. Much truer is getting on with my own way. It's not all about you, you know. Or me. We each think ourselves the central character, but sometimes one can be a minor figure even in one's own story."

She had cast off the final row of her knitting and it matched almost precisely with the length of yarn remaining. She double knotted the dangler, snipped it, and shook out the finished handiwork.

It was a large, lightweight, double afghan in a riot of soft earth colors—russets and ambers, ochres and olives—shot through with indigos the shade of blue gentians in summer, purples rich as the rock-core of an amethyst geode, and shimmering strands of pearlwhite mohair.

It was a comforter.

"For you," she smiled, "for dreaming stories. Mind you, it's only a blanket now. But one side is open, see? It's up to you, what you stuff it with in winter. Then it can be a real comforter."

He had wept on burying his mother, and once afterward

on losing another woman. Then, waking from last night's dream, he had discovered the salt was flowing from his own eyes. Now tears of deliverance streamed down his grown man's face.

He took the comforter and clasped it tightly.

"What if I don't know what materials to stuff it with? I have no knowledge, no wisdom … What if I'm not ready?"

"All I can tell you is this: *For knowledge, add. For wisdom, subtract*. In any event, now is as ready as it ever gets. You think *I'm* ready to be some kind of 'elder'? Hah! Yet here I am, next in sagacity line, tagged—while still searching for an elder to teach me how to manage this next part!"

"But … what if I can't find enough stories? I can't even grasp how it is I'm in the stories I'm *in*."

"Oh, you'd best get used to that."

"How can I believe I'm capable of this?"

"It would be arrogant to believe that. And stupid not to."

He reached for her hand.

"I am still *lost*. I have no compass."

She took his hand in both of hers.

"Oh, my friend. *When you are this close to the lodestone, no compass ever works*."

They had talked all night, and dawn was leaking grey in at the windows.

She yawned.

"Go to bed. This has been a long night."

"How can I sleep?"

"Easily. You're spent. All that screaming. Besides, you have work ahead of you. You need to rest. So do I." She rose. So did he, quickly, wary she might vanish on the spot.

"You're ready," she repeated, taking him by the shoulders.

Years later, as an old, old man, he would remember her eyes as she looked into him.

"Listen for the smallest sounds. Peer closely to find the story you sense is there," she whispered, "or stand back far enough: it's all of a piece. Then pass it on. You're already there. You don't fear meaninglessness. And you do know how to play."

She went to the sink and rinsed out their cups. Stunned, he stood watching. Then she bustled off down the hall as she had so many nights before.

He followed like a stray animal, woebegone. But he could follow only so far. When she firmly shut the door to her room he was forced to turn into his.

There he flung himself down on the bed, still a tangle of linens from his nightmare. He clutched the comforter and heard one howl rip itself from his throat.

Then late morning sun streamed across his eyes. *Here* was back.

He remembered.

How could he have slept? He rushed out to the hall, calling for her. He ran to the kitchen.

The pot of brewing tea was still warm, wrapped in its tea cozy on the stove. There was a fresh-baked loaf of bread beside the knife on the cutting board.

The Yarner was gone.

He ran out to the stoop and peered at the alley. The neighbor three houses down was sweeping his walkway as he always did at this hour, secure in his own story. No one else stirred.

He could envision her familiar shape, walking out through autumn toward the year's end—flat, strong shoes and loose-fitting trousers, one of her bright, knitted tunics; a jacket or cloak slung over her shoulder, along with a small bag. She would travel light. Head high, striding off as briskly as a sturdy staff and the limp bestowed by that aching hip permitted—into the void.

Perhaps, he thought, she had stopped for one look back along the side alleyway, at the house that boasted as its sole distinction the pear tree out front, where for so long she could have been found sitting on the stoop, watching the light change, feeding breadcrumbs to the finches, and sometimes, if in the mood when importuned, feeding a story to a hungry listener.

He slumped down on the top step. Her absence was a sickness in him so full it left room only for fear, as if he were a child.

Still.

Still, buried in that rich loam of misery, a seed was breaking open. A tendril of excitement.

How merciless life was.

He hated it.

It felt like a betrayal. It intruded into missing her, it violated his grief. He tried to conjure her snapping *Nonsense, get on with it*. But he was haunted by the unsaid. They'd never even really discussed her Last Speaker yarn! Now he was remembering all the things he had meant to say, all the places of the mind he had meant to talk with her about, all the paths that had led him, so late, to her house—

Her house.

The rooms he'd never been in.

Not that she'd ever forbidden entrance, but neither had she invited him in when she would disappear into one. In all this time his sense of the house revolved around his room, the kitchen and hearth, the library, the garden, the stoop—and his invention of her room. But he had also played a solitary game, imagining what the other rooms contained.

He'd originally furnished one as a sort of attic with old

furniture and dusty knickknacks, then scrapped that: she was not a knickknack person. He conceived of one as a bright solarium, its moist air heavy with green smells, where seedlings and plants flowered year long. Now he wondered if one room might be strewn with scribbled star maps: perhaps the son's old room. None of it would shock him any more. He believed her capable not of anything, but of many things, most of which he could not envision.

Could not envision *yet*, he thought. Missing her had for the moment receded, because he could go in and find not her but clues about her. He could unlock her mysteries, perhaps. He could freely explore her house.

His house. He actually found himself grinning.

But immediately he became intimidated by the length of the hall beyond his room—and the number of doors along it. He ceased counting at twelve, dumbfounded by the sight of what looked to be that many more doors ahead. Moreover, the discovery of two back staircases—one leading up and one down—paralyzed his adventures. From outside the house, from the street or garden, there was no evidence of a cellar or upper floors. True, a second (or third?) floor would have been obscured by the cluster of trees and buildings that backed onto the garden. But who could have imagined this humble house was so expansive, stretching up, down, backward, and branching into who knew how many rooms? *Explore all the rooms*, she'd said, *You'll be surprised*.

He retreated to the familiarity of his own room and reflected on this. The house was itself a story, then? Or a collection of stories, opening into each other?

What had the Yarner said that very first day?

"Every second, stories unfold all over the place. Some are unfolding as they happen, some haven't happened yet, some never will—and that turns out to be the story. There are stories nested inside stories, with more nested inside *them*, out past infinity. And they *keep* unfolding, continuously, simultaneously, skeins living along the same yarn. You can spot one at a time, and sometimes, very rarely, you can glimpse a multitude of them, swarming—though you can never see both the individual tale and the swarm at the same moment."

He scrambled to his feet and rushed out to the front stoop again, where he stood still, looking, listening, noticing.

Why *was* that one branch twisted just so—did it grow that way, or did a storm contort it? Who did plant the tree, why a pear, and why here? What could one imagine through the eyes of the jay in flight? His brain was filling with tales that buzzed at him from this alley, city, world, universe.

How many other clues were waiting to be discovered, in the yarns or for their making? The List Keeper—the adopted daughter? Daki's star-gazing schoolmaster friend—the astronomer son?

And what about his own life?

"Yarns often reflect conditions affecting a yarner. As if it were possible to bring outsiders in by bringing the inside out," she had said.

Why wonder what secrets his mother never got to tell him?

"It's all there in the yarns," she had said, "Imagination can conceal while it reveals, but sooner or later, everything gets used."

Letters forming sentences, clues assembling a message, marble fragments tugging together like iron filings toward a magnet.

"When you are this close to the lodestone, no compass ever works."

Yarns knitting toward a pattern, a comforter, a life.

The secrets! Who his grandfather really was, who his mother was, who he himself was!

His grandfather was Lobaak, his mother, Lobaa! He was the child with whom his mother fled to freedom from those who would imprison them, either because they feared the child or adored him, and because Lobaa knew neither choice would let him discover who *he* wanted to be. *It's all there in the yarns.*

The Word Worker! The echo-self from another dimension: Tayyaq! The character in a different story, so engaged in saving the world he would do not what was necessary but what was possible. The road not taken, the man he might have been … the man he might yet become? Surely not. He had chosen this path, turned from that type of power. Otherwise, the Yarner would never have left him as the inheritor.

Or would she? *It's up to you*, she had said.

That was it. The burden. The decision was ongoing. He would have to keep deciding, every day of his life. There was no knowing how it would end but by living it. His eyes burned with tears. Salt. *It's all in the yarns.*

The cat came trotting down the alley toward him, breaking his reverie.

"Good morning, Cat," he smiled sadly. "I'm sorry, I never learned your name, or if you even deign to have one."

He knew his own name now, though. He was The Yarner, and that recognition flooded him with a sense of power. If freedom had been the theme of the former Yarner, power might be his. He made a fist and raised it triumphantly.

Then he lowered his arm and stared at the fist.

The yarns, the house—they were his only for a span, like the baton borne by runners in a relay race. He was the caretaker, and he must tend house and yarning until his inheritors appeared in turn to free him. It would never be finished. He thought of how tiny sea animals communally construct a reef over thousands of years, how generations of nameless masons and stonecutters and glaziers erect a cathedral's spires across centuries.

Power volunteered. Slowly, he unclenched his fist.

"Mine for now," the Yarner softly acknowledged, terrified, lighthearted, "Mine to do."

He turned and faced his house. A cup of tea, he suddenly thought. Some toast. How comforting that sounded! He entered his house and went to the kitchen.

A flutter in the morning breeze caught his attention. It was a piece of paper on the kitchen table, weighted down by the vase holding a single late russet-orange daisy with a sable center. His heart lurched against his ribs. She had left him a note!

It wasn't a note. It was a list. Only thirteen words.

Remember the cat.

The rest is up to you.

Thank you, my dear.

*If you would like to know more about Spinifex Press,
write to us for a free catalogue, visit our website,
follow us on social media or email us for further information.*

Spinifex Press
PO Box 105
Mission Beach QLD 4852
Australia

www.spinifexpress.com.au
women@spinifexpress.com.au